BIG
Furry
DEAL

CELIA KYLE

NEW YORK TIMES BESTSELLING AUTHOR

Panther shifter Millie Walker is finally free, finally knows her real name, and finally… has a mate? Well, crap.

For Millie, having a mate is a horrible, no good, he'll end up very dead, bad idea. She's got what some refer to as a "control problem." In other words: she has no control and that's her problem. So, she stays away from others, keeps to herself, and generally tries not to kill people. Except the pride Prima—Maya—has this "awesomesauce" idea and suddenly Millie's at a pride picnic surrounded by people… and then she meets her mate. Her tall, delicious, please-may-I-lick-you-from-head-to-toe mate. Now she prays her powers don't suddenly decide Wyatt is better off six feet under.

Lion shifter Wyatt Dane knows he's not the kind of man who takes a mate. His own mother proved he wasn't worth loving. But then he meets Millie. Millie with her fiery hair, generous curves, and dangerous powers. He tries to resist her, forces himself to reject her, but then she returns and he realizes he can't let her go. Her powers will just have to figure out how to deal with his presence. He's keeping her. Period.

But someone from her past didn't get the "she's mated" memo and he's determined to have her, no matter the cost.

Warning: Big Furry Deal contains kick ass violence, some potentially trigger content (what do we expect from the bad guy), and copious hilarity. Be prepared for laughing, crying, and cringing. As always, curvy women rock, boys drool-girls rule, and your mileage may vary.

CHAPTER *one*

"You got opinions, I got opinions, we've all got opinions. The thing is, your opinions can bite my as— Ahem. Never mind." — Maya O'Connell, Prima of the Ridgeville Pride and woman who loves her children but wishes they would go away sometimes. Like when she's ready tell someone to bite her ass.

Millie sat on her bed and traced the blue, swirling lines bordering the paper and stroked the raised seal at the bottom of the page. The pattern filled the edges, and she let her fingers dance over the design. Her touch stuttered when she reached the top, tips trembling as she read the words.

Amelia Beth Walker.

Amelia. Beth. Walker.

Ameliabethwalker.

State of Nebraska. Certificate of Birth.

She had a name now. A true name. Not one thrown at her during captivity.

Amelia Beth Walker.

Born October 28, 1979.

Millie leaned against the headboard and dug through her mind, drifting deeper and deeper as she sought her oldest memory. She ached to find a time when Amelia Beth Walker was a name she recognized.

She craved memories of her childhood, of a time when she laughed and played. She wanted to go back to those two years she spent with her parents, with her twin brother... Her mind sought out remembrances not tainted by Alistair's touch.

Her hands trembled, the page shaking in her grip, and her tenuous control wavered. Fighting for those memories always brought forth the same reaction within her body.

Damn it, she couldn't lose control. Not now. She knew her real name. She wanted to know herself. Again, she looked and yet again stumbled across abuse after abuse. The paper in her hand fell to the sheets and the memories and pain came. She pulled her knees up, wrapping her arms around them, slowly rocking, slowly rocking.

Inside her head, she was back in that underground compound— prison—one of Alistair McCain's hidden lairs deep in a mountain. Alistair, the leader of Freedom—an anti-establishment shifter group—was dead and the council was repurposing his holdings.

The cold walls encompassed them, five women who clung to sanity by a thread. They lingered in the living area where it was easy to see who came and went. So many new faces come to save them. So many more.

Millie ran a hand through her hair, fingers tangling on the strands, and then the low ding of the elevator drew her attention. She listened to the whirring gears and shifting bolts of the metal box as she wondered who could be coming back.

She sensed it wasn't *him*. It wasn't *that* male.

But the two people about to step off the elevator shouldn't be in the compound. It was an intruder—one of her saviors?—and... one of *them*, one of Alistair's men. She recognized him. Her power whipped at her, the Sensitive part of her rushing forward in its twisted and perverted form.

The doors to the elevator eased open, the metal panels separating slowly to grant this newcomer's entrance. Millie held her breath. Her power lashed at her, growing with her unease. It slithered through her, demanding to be released upon the familiar, unwanted presence. She opened her mouth and drew in a breath, scenting the air. Yes. *Males.*

Now it was no longer a matter of allowing her abilities free reign. That ball of rage that had forever been a part of her rushed forward and stole control.

One booted foot came into view, bringing a massive shifter male along with it. No, no, no. She couldn't have another male in her space.

Her Sensitive abilities reacted to her panic.

The stranger, she didn't know. Was he one of the good guys?

The power didn't care if its victims had nothing to do with Alistair McCain. It craved vengeance.

No, she pleaded, he wasn't a bad male, he wouldn't harm them, he wouldn't…

Invisible strands burst from her body and raced through the compound's living room. They were aimed at this man. In less than a second, her power struck him. It dug into his mind, pulling and tugging at bits and pieces of him.

Next she hunted the pain centers in his brain, dug deep and gathered every one in her ghostly hand. And yanked. His entire body spasmed as she overloaded him with agony.

So much pain invaded the other that not a shout or scream escaped his lips before he lay prone on the ground, unconscious.

The power was pleased.

Another tendril of rage-filled power flowed from her body, slinking through the room, hunting the other being: Alistair's man.

He would know the pain he gave her all these years. All the times they stood in Alistair's group, pawing and taking what they wanted. *Men.*

He stepped out of the elevator and fell to his knees, his cuffed hands covered his ears as if he could block its passage inside his skull. Bulges and bubbles stretched skin over the cranial bones. Portions of his skull rose and fell.

Millie was horrified by the action while her power was not. It felt vindicated, overjoyed at hurting a male before it hurt them again. One last push to protect her.

Millie rolled into a ball and screamed as the man's head exploded into fine red mist.

Her own scream brought her back from the nightmare. Her heart raced with anxiety. When she killed a prisoner that day, she had been drugged and weakened from Alistair's abuse. Now after eight months of freedom—six months in the Freedom compound and two in Ridgeville—she was strong and healthy, and she worried about the damage she could cause.

Millie closed her eyes and took a deep breath. The last thing she wanted to do was hurt one of her saviors. Saviors...

After more years than she could count, she had saviors.

No, not more than she could count. She picked up the birth certificate again. Thirty-two years. She'd been kidnapped at two and spent thirty years in Alistair's clutches.

How could anyone know she had the abilities of a powerful Sensitive when she was still a toddler? Through the years, she came to learn a

Sensitive could influence any shifter, and was able to both soothe and destroy another's mind.

It was times like these that she hated her Sensitive abilities. For the average female shifter, being a Sensitive was a blessing and occasionally an annoyance. They were born with the ability to glide into another shifter's mind and control their beast. A simple thought soothed the animal and a little more effort allowed the Sensitive to control another's mind.

Unfortunately for Millie, she was stronger than most. Or rather, stronger than any. And through the years, all she endured day in and day out corrupted her abilities, molded and reshaped them into what there were now.

Dangerous. Uncontrollable. Deadly.

She reminded the power that they were free, fed, and had a roof over their head. Evil males didn't linger in the shadows waiting for a chance to abuse her. They weren't hiding around corners with tranquilizer guns aimed at her. They weren't waiting for the drugs to take hold so they could...

In Ridgeville, there was no reason to be on guard. No reason to hunt for its next target. She prayed it'd listen, prayed it'd ease back. She held her breath, waiting to see how it'd react.

It grumbled and retreated, slithered back inside her and behind the mental walls she'd built to contain that part of herself. She breathed a sigh of relief. That part of her grew stronger as her physical body regained its strength.

Millie looked inside herself, pushed past the dark cloud of her power and on toward her inner-panther. The cat paced, snarling and growling at the ball of ghost-like power, but did not go near it.

It was always the same, the two always living separate lives inside her body. It wasn't supposed to be this way, though. Yes, shifters often referred to their animals as individual beings, and in some ways they were. But for someone like her, for a Sensitive who had abilities others did not, it was dangerous.

With her body torn into three, she was afraid she'd destroy herself.

"Mil-lie!" Maya's bellow vibrated the entire house. The Ridgeville Prima's roar caught her off guard and her power shot to the surface in an agonizing rush, anticipating her need for protection. The lioness must have let herself into the house Millie shared with the Mastin sisters. The owner, Gina, recently mated and moved away, leaving the place empty and perfect for Millie and the sisters.

"Damn it, *not now*," Millie whispered to herself and pushed back, shoved the hate deeper into her body and wrapped it up tight. "She's the freaking Prima. The mate to the Prime and one of the people who can kick our ass to the curb."

"I'm also the Queen of Booblandia, but whatevs." Maya's voice filled the room. "And talking to yourself can be a sign of schizophrenia. Are you schizophrenic?"

Millie smiled as she rolled off the bed and turned toward the bedroom door. "No, not schizophrenic."

Maya narrowed her eyes. "Are you sure? I bet a schizophrenic person would say they weren't schizophrenic to avoid wearing a straitjacket in a non-bondage-happy-fun-times way."

Millie rolled her eyes. "I'm sure."

The Prima smiled wide. "Good. That means you can have multiple personalities instead. Because then I'd get two, or more, new best friends instead of one."

Millie tilted her head to the side, confusion filling her. "Huh?"

Maya rolled her eyes. "I swear, does no one follow a conversation here?" she huffed. "Gina-the-whore mated Gavin-the-dog, which left me down a best friend. So, you're here now, and you *talk*," Maya scrunched her nose. "Not that I'm saying anything bad about the

6

Mastin sisters and their not talking thing. I mean, I'm not a totally insensitive bitch, right?" She waved her hands. "Anyway, I'll apologize later. But what this all means is you take her place. Except you-you were supposed to be a *new* bestie. So now I'm down *two* besties. And *that* means you need to have multiple personalities and take up both spots." Happiness and excitement filled Maya's features. "Are you picking up what I'm putting down?"

Millie sifted through the babble. Okay, she knew Gina (a Ridgeville lioness) recently mated Gavin (a dog, er, fox and brother to another Ridgeville pride member). Which left this home empty and a Gina-sized hole in Maya's life. But then there was the "you" and the "you-you" and...

"No." Millie shook her head. "Not so much."

Maya heaved a put-upon sigh. "None of you *listen*. Okay, let's do this again." The Prima straightened and held up a finger. "Gina-the-whore—"

"For the love of—Maya!" Alex, the Prime and Maya's mate, yelled. His voice echoed through the house, causing the Prima to jump.

Millie wished that was all it did to her. No, the enraged part of her burst free of its moorings and shoved against her control. It sliced through layer after layer of her bindings and stretched the last that kept it within her body.

The memories made it too raw, too powerful. If only she'd had an hour, half an hour... hell, with a few minutes of quiet time, she could have ensured it was tied up tight and ready for visitors.

"*What?*" The Prima seemed ignorant of her struggles.

"We're late!"

Maya scoffed and turned toward the hall to yell at her mate. "We can't be late. We're the most important people there."

Millie struggled to breathe. Her birth certificate slipped from her fingers, and she fisted her hands, digging her nails into the soft flesh of her palms. Her abilities scraped the last layer of her mental walls. It sensed Alex in the house. Part of it recognized him as a mated male, as someone who'd helped them, but another thought drifted forward. Even a mated male could beat a woman. Even a mated male could forc—

Panic set in, her heart racing as her lungs fought to bring air in and out of her body. Sweat beaded on her forehead, peppering her in the salty fluid. The scent of blood soon joined the others in the room, and the Prima's gaze swung back to her.

Millie ignored the worry and shock in Maya's gaze. She had her own crap.

Please, please, please. She wasn't sure what she was begging for. Relief? Forgiveness? An end?

She was so tired, so tired of living this way day in and day out. For one moment she'd like to not have to worry about accidentally harming someone.

"*Maya.*" Alex wasn't giving up.

Maya ignored him and approached her. This was a different version of Maya, one that didn't have a ready smile and obnoxious jokes on her lips. This one was worried with her brow scrunched and concern in her gaze. "Millie? Hon?"

She shook her head and took a step back. That part of her still fighting to break free attacked her to get at the one who'd scared them. Damn it. She'd knocked Harding on his ass months ago. At the time, he'd been down for the count for a day or two. Since being in Ridgeville, she'd grown stronger. She wasn't sure what would happen if her power struck out now.

She remembered the glory of Harding's nerves sliding over her palms as she manipulated his mind. It'd reveled in the flavors of his pain. The power had a taste for it now and she didn't want to see what else it would enjoy.

Millie eased closer to the window. It opened to the backyard. She'd run, beg her cat to take control and carry them away from the house. She'd run and run and fight to keep away from everyone.

"Millie, it's okay." Maya took another step forward.

"Stop." She held up a bloodied hand, trying to keep the Prima at bay.

"No, you're not going to hurt me. You're not going to hurt anyone." The Prima eased closer.

"Maya…"

"*Maya!*" Alex's roar had Millie jumping and scurrying back until she came up against the far wall.

Maya's cat reacted to her mate's demand. But instead of cowering or becoming afraid, it was obvious the Prima was easing toward enraged. Golden fur slithered over the woman's arms and legs while her eyes flashed a bright amber. She whirled away from Millie and stomped to the bedroom door.

Okay, she was leaving. Good. Millie tried to soothe her abilities, assure it that with Maya's departure, the male would leave their domain. It didn't care. It remembered the touch of Harding's mind and it wanted to see if Alex would be the same. What it'd be like to tug on all of those other lovely nerve centers.

The Prima stuck her head out of the room and let loose a roar of her own. "For the love of *fur*, I'm trying to keep her from blowing your brains out! A little patience is appreciated!" The woman stepped back into Millie's bedroom and then slammed the door so hard the walls shook. "Though why I'm saving your stupid, little pea-sized brain is beyond me." Maya paused for a moment and looked to her. "It's because he has a nice, big cock—"

"Maya!" Alex interrupted again.

9

"I was gonna say cocker spaniel you big, ungrateful ass!" Maya shook her head and whispered. "I meant cock. Just don't tell him."

"Ass... ass... ass..." The word was repeated over and over by identical voices and Maya winced. The Prima's twins, East and West, had heard her. Then again, the entire block probably heard her.

"Damn, I was supposed to stop cursing. That's gonna earn me a spanking." The twinkle in the Prima's eyes told Millie the spanking would be welcome.

Shock filled Millie, though she wasn't sure why each of the Prima's outbursts still surprised her. After two months in Ridgeville, she should have been used to the loud arguments between the ruling couple. Loud arguments which, from reports, ended in even louder make up sessions.

The twin's chorus drifted down the hallway and the happiness filling each word crept into her mind. The delight wrapped around her raging power and its need to attack was blunted by their joy. That was one thing it recognized. Children were a near perfect barometer when it came to judging others and the twins were filled with pure delight.

Her abilities stalled in their attempt to break free, stuttering, and it gave Millie the chance she needed. She mentally burst forward, intent on locking her power tightly once again.

Alex's growl traveled up the stairs, but at least he didn't yell. That cloud inside her mind roiled and bubbled, but didn't fight for freedom. It knew the cubs were in the house and accepted its bindings. The power allowed itself to be eased into the back of her head and out of sight. That part of her was always quick to lash out, but retreated when faced with an innocent.

"Oh, look at that." Maya stepped closer, her gaze intent on Millie. "Kidlets appear and your eyes go back to normal. Suhweet! I knew I was right." The Prima shook her ass and waved her arms in the air in what Millie supposed was some sort of dancing. "Go me, it's my birthday, I was right, and they were *wrong*. Yeah!"

It then morphed into some weird, full body… thing… and she wondered if the Prima had gone into convulsions. "Uh, Maya?"

Maya froze. "Huh. Sorry. I was just excited. Wanna know why? C'mon, ask why. Ask. Do it." The Prima bounced on her toes.

Life in Ridgeville was just… weird. She didn't want to know why, but she couldn't tell the Prima no. "Um, why?"

"Because you won't hurt the babies." The smile was triumphant and slowly slipped to confusion. "No, wait. Went to the grand finale without any foreplay." She waved her hands. "Do over. You're coming to Honor's graduation, and it will be safe *because you won't hurt the babies*." Maya jerked her head in a quick nod. "Got it right that time. High five."

The rapid pounding of tiny feet on the stairs preceded the appearance of the O'Connell twins. They were little balls of destruction and no one doted, or yelled at them, more than Maya.

"Graduation?" There was no way.

She'd barely left the house since she'd moved to Ridgeville. In the beginning, she attempted to socialize with the pride, but her power was too protective, too strong. It whipped and struck whenever she felt threatened, which happened way too often for other people's comfort. All of her training, her therapy, and her rehab occurred within Gina's home.

She couldn't wander out of the door and to Honor's graduation. Yes, Honor was important to Maya. The girl was one of her guard's younger sisters and insanely smart, but there was no way Millie could—

Millie's thoughts were cut off by the sudden appearance of East—or was it West—in her arms. Maya shoved the small, wiggling boy into her hands and then stepped back with a wide smile on her face.

"There ya go. The kid is still alive which means you're coming. Graduation with a lot of blah, blah, blah." Maya made a talking motion with her hands. "And then lotsa food at the pride house. You get to be babysitter, and everyone else stays conscious and undead. Win-win."

Worry eased into Millie, concern over the people she'd be around as well as the cubs shoved into her care. She couldn't say no, but she didn't want to say yes either. "Maybe we should start smaller?"

"Smaller? Well, Elise's pup is barely two months old, so I doubt her mate, Brute, is about to let Katie outta his sight. Maddy's cub, Brody, is six months old now. He might work." Maya snapped her fingers. "Dam-ang, but he can't walk which means you won't be running after him, and you need cardio."

Millie concerned herself with leaving people brain dead, and Maya was worried about… cardio.

Tiny hands slapped her cheeks, and she allowed the boy to direct her attention to him. "Ass… Ass ass ass…"

"Maya!" Alex's roar shook the entire house, vibrating the walls and floor and the tremors invaded her body.

Fear engulfed her, filled her body with anxiety as she waited for her powers to respond except… except they didn't. That dark part of her didn't make a sound as growls and snarls from Alex drifted up the stairs. No, her cloud of rage was content and soothed by the giggling, cursing child smacking her cheeks. It remained vigilant and wary, but no longer felt the need to lash out without cause. For the first time in longer than she knew, she breathed worry free.

"Okay." She didn't tear her gaze from the cub.

12

"Okay?" Maya's voice was filled with hope and excitement.

"Yeah, okay." Millie nodded. She might regret it later, everyone might regret it later. But as long as she was able to keep one of the children in her arms, she'd go.

"Suhweet!" The Prima pumped her fist in the air. "I got a babysitter."

CHAPTER *two*

"I don't always have to be right, I just need to make sure you realize you're always wrong. Are we on the same page here? No? Lemme get you a bookmark." — Maya O'Connell, Prima of the Ridgeville Pride and publisher of the award winning book: *Maya is Always Right So Shaddup.*

Wyatt leaned against the fence that encircled the pride house backyard and kept his attention on the cluster fuck in progress across the way. The yard overflowed with people of varying ages, mostly pride members and some not. Honor Mauer, one of the guard's younger sisters, graduated high school a few hours ago. And since Maya always looked for an excuse to have a party, Honor's graduation was the perfect reason to throw a shindig. Now they were all hanging out, drinking beers, eating hotdogs and enjoying time together.

Well, most of them were enjoying time together.

Grayson, Alex's Second, stood brooding on one side of the yard, glaring at all the newly graduated boys surrounding Honor. All of 'em vied for her attention, some more blatantly than others, but all of them flirting with the young lioness.

In turn, Honor constantly looked past the boys to glare at Grayson.

Wyatt couldn't wait to see those two clash. From the moment Grayson let the maybe-mate secret out of the bag, the whole pride had watched them circle each other. Grayson was a lot older than her and Honor had a lot of growing up to do, but the two snarled at each other like cats and dogs. Even if they were both cats.

A shift of air and crunch of nearby grass announced someone's approach. He turned his head enough to catch sight of his visitor. Harding eased beside him, handing over a beer as he leaned against the fence, and they both stared and waited for the show.

Wyatt brought the bottle to his lips and tipped it back, enjoying the bitter brew as it slid over his taste buds. Nothing better than a cold beer on a hot day. He swallowed a mouthful and lowered the bottle. "Do you think he knows Honor's going to college in England?"

Harding grunted.

He shouldn't be surprised at the man's form of communication. They'd been through a hell of a lot together. Harding had joined the pride at sixteen. Alone. Tortured, scarred, and kicked out of his pride.

Wyatt didn't carry scars like his friend. At least not on the outside. On the inside, however…

Alex rounded the corner of the house and pause as he hunted for someone. As soon as the Prime's gaze landed on Grayson, Alex frowned.

"Looks like he'll know soon enough," Wyatt murmured.

Alex went to Grayson and leaned into the lion. Then he saw the change come over the man. Annoyance gave way to pure rage and a half-shift burst through Grayson in less than a blink. The man's roar echoed through the yard, silencing all conversation and causing everyone to freeze.

Yeah, the pride's Second was pissed. Thankfully, it wasn't at him.

Grayson bolted across the yard, shoving aside unmoving pride members and random guests until he stood before Honor. In one

16

great heave, the newly graduated lioness was tossed over Grayson's shoulder. Without another word, the male strode off, Honor's screeches filling the air in his wake.

"Bet he knows now," Harding stated the obvious.

"Yup." He took another swig of beer.

The moment Grayson and Honor hit the tree line and ducked out of sight, the party resumed. Brute manned the grill while his mate Elise sat nearby, cuddling their newborn fox pup, Katie. The pup was a little over two months old, and both parents refused to let the little girl out of their sight.

In the shade of a large maple tree, Elly and Deuce sat at a picnic table. Poor Elly was as big as a house, and Deuce had been running himself ragged trying to keep up with her cravings. They'd all be glad when Elly popped.

On the other side of the yard, Maddy, Carly, and Maya congregated around a tray of veggies. Veggies. At a party for a carnivore. They were letting way too many herbivores into the pride.

"Where's Tess?"

Harding tipped his bottle toward the pride house. "Trying to hide. I figure I'll give her five more minutes and then I'll go in after her."

The man tried to conceal his grin behind his bottle, but Wyatt caught it. Harding wouldn't mind hunting down his mate. Not one bit.

The thought left a familiar, empty pang in his chest. What would it be to have someone like that? Someone by his side and filled with unconditional love.

A memory bolted forward and struck him before he had a chance to shut it down.

You're nothing but a worthless monster...

17

The words cut deep, slicing into him as they had all those years ago. He couldn't figure out if it was worse now, or then. At the age of five, he hadn't understood, not really, but today was a different story. Thirty years after the fact and still he wondered.

He shoved away the blossoming jealousy. No sense in being jealous when there wasn't anything he could do to change the hand he'd been dealt.

Some males had mates. Some didn't.

Kids ran through the yard, racing this way and that, giggling and laughing. Half of them wore their fur, while the other half was hardly dressed and scrambled through the grass with bare feet. Kids being kids.

He wondered if he'd ever been like that.

Then he remembered he had. But that'd been before. Before he started kindergarten. Before he met a loudmouthed kid. Before he discovered his...

He shoved all that away too.

"It's been five minutes." Harding tossed his beer into a nearby trash can. "Ignore the screams." The man shot him a grin and then jogged toward the house.

"Damn." He took a swig of his beer and frowned when it turned up empty. "Shit."

"Shit!"

"Shit shit!"

Double shit. The twin's voices hit him from opposite sides, their echoing chorus surrounding him as they giggled and repeated the curse.

18

"Shit… shit… shit… shit…" They danced around, ducking beneath the fence to pop up in front of him.

"Stop that. You're gonna get me in trouble with your daddy." He ruffled East's hair and tugged a lock of West's.

Half the pride couldn't tell them apart, but Wyatt could. He'd always wanted cubs, so they were something he kept his eye on. He was watchful, ready to take care of them if need be. His lion couldn't wait to be a father, even if his human half was just as determined to live alone. His whole life was a constant battle, but it was normal. A part of him.

Because monsters shouldn't have children.

East wrapped his small arms around his leg and stepped onto Wyatt's foot. West soon followed.

"Walk!"

"Wanna walk!"

Wyatt grinned and gave in to the two boys. They were filled with life, filled with joy, and there wasn't much he *wouldn't* give them. He took one step, and then another, pretending to stumble on the third, which caused another round of screaming laughs. Chuckling, he kept it up, stomping and play-growling at the cubs as he moved toward the picnic table.

Their little claws came out to play, sharp tips digging into his jeans, but he didn't care. The small cuts would be healed in moments. What did a little discomfort matter when compared to their delight?

Not a thing.

Twenty feet from the picnic table, Maya caught sight of them. Her cheerful expression fled, the flush of her laughs draining to leave her pale. "Easton? Weston? What are you doing with Wyatt?"

The boys froze, their tiny bodies tense. "Uh…"

The Prima bolted up from the picnic table and scrambled atop the wood surface as she raised her voice to a roar. "Alex? Millie?"

Wyatt furrowed his brow and looked around as well. He wasn't sure what Millie looked like since he'd never met the woman. There were stories about her being dangerous, that her time with Freedom had twisted her Sensitive abilities in knots. He figured everyone had their demons, a few more hazardous than others, and she'd come out when she was good and ready. From what he'd heard, she was skittish and refused to leave Gina's house, but Maya cajoled her into attending Honor's graduation.

"Alex!" Maya's voice overrode everyone's in the yard, her fear evident in her tone. The cubs, sensing their mom's worry, released him and scampered toward their mother. Carly was quick to step in and gather them close.

"What?" The Prime strode toward them, the crowd parting to allow him to pass. "What's wrong?"

"I have the boys." Maya pointed at East and West.

"And…" Alex waved a hand at her to continue and then he too stilled, color draining. "Shit. Where was she last seen?"

Maya shook her head. "I don't know."

"*Fuck.*" Alex ran a hand through his hair. "Get everyone in the house. Keep them there. Do not let anyone out. I'll find her."

"But she could—" Maya hopped down from the table and stepped toward Alex.

"Which is something you should have considered before you bulldozed everyone and brought her to the picnic," Alex snapped.

The Prime's anger hit the air first, the scent of scorching heat filling his nose. It intensified with each breath, rage forcing it to burn even hotter. The sharp tang of fear joined the maelstrom and Wyatt choked on the stench. Fur sprouted from Alex's arms and his shirt

20

stretched taut across his shoulders and chest. The Prime's shift was nearly upon him with the tumultuous feelings coursing through his veins.

"I just wanted…" Tears glistened in Maya's eyes.

Wyatt couldn't keep quiet any longer. He didn't know what the hell was going on, but he wasn't about to let his Prime walk into anything Maya thought would be dangerous. Alex led their pride, he was important to their happiness; Wyatt… was not.

"Prime? Is there something I can do?"

Alex shook his head. "No, it's my responsibility. I shouldn't have allowed her to come. I'll find her."

"She was cooped up too long. We're overreacting. She's fine and having a good time and… Oh, shit. There she is."

Wyatt followed the direction of Maya's gaze and watched a woman race to the tree line. The breeze lifted and fanned her red hair like dancing fire. It trailed after her, chasing her into the forest.

His lion rushed forward, demanding he hunt the female, pin her to the ground, and mark her with their scent. She was beautiful with lush curves and gorgeous, pale skin.

He didn't wait for Alex's order or Maya's demand. No, his cat wanted to run the prey down. He took off after her, first striding and then breaking into a gentle jog before shifting into a ground-eating run. He chased after her, his lion urging him *faster, push harder*. For some reason, it needed the woman like its next breath. She had to be in their arms. Now.

The closer he drew, the clearer she became. Shorts clung to her rounded ass and curved hips while a fitted T-shirt was snug against her upper-body.

Her scent drifted to him on the breeze, the seductive flavors of sweet honeysuckle and melon teased him, tormented him with the promise of heaven. Shit, his cock went rock hard, and his lion roared in approval of her. The female. Their female.

Fuck. He should stop, should put on the brakes and run as far and fast as he could in the other direction. But first… First he'd catch her because that's what the Prime wanted. He'd touch her for a moment and then disappear. He'd leave and find a new pride and forget he'd ever met her because any woman deserved so much better than him.

Wyatt must have made a sound because she slid to a stop, sneakers slipping over the grass for a brief moment before she stilled. The woman spun on him, holding out her hands as if to keep him at bay.

"Back up. Just. Back. Up." Her voice was hoarse, scratchy, and sweat beaded on her temple. "It hurts." He tasted her pain on his tongue and his cat fought to break free and kill whatever hurt her. "Please stay away." The words broke off with a rough sob.

Wyatt mirrored her position, holding up his hands. "Look, Alex wants you. I'm here to…" *Claim you. Make you mine. Tie us together forever.*

No, none of the above.

The woman shook her head. "No, I'm pretty sure he *doesn't* want me. The exact opposite." She took a step back, and he stepped forward. "You don't understand. I need to go."

"And I can't let you. Alex wants you."

She shook her head. "No, you're not listening. I—" She gasped and clutched her head, curling in on herself with a deep moan.

Fuck it. She belonged to him, didn't she? He bolted forward and caught her as she fell to the ground, groaning and whimpering. "Easy, I've got you."

The lion growled in worry, but also chuffed in approval. It was happy they were at least caring for their mate even if his human half didn't want her. She didn't seem to want him either. Which… hurt.

Badly. As close as they were, she should have sensed they belonged together. Yet, she didn't cling to him like a mate should. She was fighting to get away.

"No, no, no…" She pushed and shoved, arms and legs flailing.

"Damn it, woman." Wyatt tightened his grip. "Sit still and I'll let you go."

Her breaths came in heaving puffs, each exhale painting him with more and more of her scent. His cock remained rock hard and ready to fill her while his cat prepared to pounce. Already the beast prowled beneath his skin, prepared to claim the lush woman in his arms.

After all these years, the lion still felt they were worthy of a mate.

Images of retreating tail lights flashed through his mind… *She didn't say goodbye.*

No, he wasn't mate material.

Just as fast as she fought, she froze, body tense. Her gaze clashed with his, bright green eyes boring into him. "I tried to fight it. I'm sorry."

The last word left her lips and a frigid breeze encompassed him. It scraped his skin and scratched his face. The shards of ice burned him with their glacial temperature, but then, they melted. The ice cold warmed and heated against his flesh, seeming to dissolve into him until he felt as if he were being stroked. Ethereal hands pet him, sliding over his body in a gentle caress. The ghostly touch had him aching for her even more and wishing they had a bed nearby… And a hell of a lot less clothes.

The woman in his arms held her breath, her attention never leaving him. Silence reigned as they stared at each other. She was sorry for something, he wasn't sure what, and he didn't want to break the spell that encompassed them.

He had his mate in his arms, and he didn't want to let her go. At least not until he had to.

Wyatt released one of her arms, brought his hand up, and stroked her cheek. "Are you okay?"

"You're alive." Awe filled her words.

"As opposed to…"

"Knocked out, coma, dead." Alex's gasping words broke the spell around them.

The woman in his arms jerked from his hold, scrambling away until ten feet separated them. "Get away, Alex."

Her anxiety, her fear and worry, tainted the air and Wyatt's lion was quick to react. He rolled to his feet in one fluid move and took two strides closer. He could be at her side in another two and in plenty of time to stop whatever threat Alex may pose. Whether he kept her or not, she was still his mate.

"Millie, it's obvious you're fine without a cub in your arms."

His mate shook her head, and he noticed the trembles and peppering of sweat had returned. Her skin shifted and bulged as if something inside were trying to push its way out. It wasn't the normal teasings of an inner-animal. It was something different, something more.

"No, I'm not. For some reason, I didn't fry this guy's brain, but you're about to find out how not-fine I am, Alex." Millie took a step back, and Wyatt followed her. "It's pushing hard, Alex. I need to get away from all of these men."

He didn't know what "it" was, but he agreed with her. She needed to get away from any male that wasn't him.

"Leave, Alex."

Except Alex took another step forward. When Millie moved to ease farther back, a bone-shattering tremble overtook her. Her balance wavered, and she stumbled, body falling to the side with a low cry.

The air shivered around him, vibrating with *something*, but he couldn't be bothered with anything but Millie. Wyatt bolted forward, ignoring Alex's order to stop and her cry to run. He wasn't about to let her collapse on the ground. He might be a mate who wasn't worth a damn, but he refused to let her get hurt under his watch.

The soft shudders turned into a razor sharp breeze when he was two feet from her. He ignored the annoying pain once again. It was obviously caused by his mate, but he couldn't have cared less. If every touch of skin on skin resulted in a brief ache, he'd happily live out the rest of his years with the hurts.

The moment she was in reach, he grabbed her, yanking her close and then swinging her into his arms. He cradled her against him, tucking her into the safe shelter of his hold. In that instant, the pain blossomed to low heat once again while the rushing breeze drifted into nothing.

Alex's shocked gaze met his, the Prime's mouth hanging wide.

His mate's next words had him wondering what he'd gotten himself into. "I didn't kill you."

"Uh," he raised his eyebrows and looked to his Prime before returning his attention to his mate. "Good?"

A ghostlike hint of darkness drifted across her eyes and then vanished as quickly as it'd appeared. "Maybe."

CHAPTER *three*

"Taking a walk in the forest should be soothing. After all, it's likely you're about to hunt something and rip it to shreds with your fangs." — Maya O'Connell, Prima of the Ridgeville Pride and a woman who wished ice cream also lived in the woods.

Millie hadn't killed him. Well, that part of her hadn't killed him. In fact, after the first caress of power against skin, it'd backed down and... welcomed him. Even weirder, when it'd tried to go after Alex, the man's presence halted the attack.

Double weird. She couldn't figure out if it was a good thing or bad. One certainty: it scared the hell out of her.

She followed him, keeping distance between them while still moving in his wake. They traveled through the forest, taking the long way to the road that led to the pride house. The last thing she wanted to do was injure anyone in the pride. Since the male seemed safe from her rogue abilities, he'd offered to take her home. Alex had agreed with the plan, and after exchanging names, they began their trek.

Millie's near dormant panther perked up as they followed him. She needed to stop referring to the male as "him." He had a name. Wyatt Dane.

He should have been named "Gorgeous." He was tall, taller than Alex, but leaner. That didn't mean he didn't hold a dominance that nearly brought her to her knees, though. No, power lurked within him, barely controlled and heavily restrained. It radiated from his skin and filled the air around him. Even her panther responded to his strength. The moment they touched, it reacted. It urged her to get closer, to wrap around the male and beg him to sink into her. Claim her.

Claim?

Millie stumbled over a root, and she held out her hands, ready to catch her weight. Except she didn't. Wyatt was there, strong arms wrapped around her, holding her above the ground.

The dark part of her stirred at the touch, but seemed to recognize the male and it quickly settled. Her cat, however, did not. It rolled to its feet in a rapid, excited rush and chuffed in greeting. The animal that normally skulked in the back of her mind and hid from every confrontation wanted to pounce, bite, and mate.

Oh, God, that's what it was. That was the delicious scent that beckoned her, the glorious aroma that had her body heating and aching for… something.

This man with his heavily muscled body, short hair and deep blue eyes belonged to her. He was her mate, her one, and the only male she could never, ever have. Her pussy didn't care, though. No, it warmed and clenched in anticipation. She felt herself grow slick with desire and Wyatt's nostrils flared as he inhaled deep. His chest expanded and then contracted for the barest of moments before filling once again.

A hardness against her hip made her realize he was affected as well. He recognized her, his body reacting to her closeness.

"Th-thank you," she whispered.

Wyatt's eyes flared gold and then settled back into a navy blue. "You're welcome."

He eased her to her feet and she took a giant step back. Touching him was a not good, very bad thing. It made her think of things she couldn't have, no matter how much she craved him.

"You okay?" Concern laced his tone, but need filled his expression.

"Fine." She nodded, even though she was anything but.

"My SUV should be another fifty yards or so. Are you going to be okay with that?"

Anger snapped in her veins. With her nerves raw from her trip down memory lane that morning and the stress of being around so many people, she immediately fell on her insecurities. The rubbing together of her thighs and the sheen of sweat coating her skin reminded her of the state of her body. Reminded her that she carried more than a few extra pounds.

It hadn't been an issue in captivity; it was hard to be concerned about body size when she spent most of her time starving. Being in the real world introduced her to any food she could imagine... and the pounds that came with it. Now she was no longer hungry, but she was also what the general public considered overweight. Eight months of freedom and already her views were skewed by the media's idea of perfection.

"Why wouldn't I? Because I'm fat?"

In a blink, he moved from five feet away to inches from her. "Fat? Never. You're gorgeous." He ran a finger along her cheek, and she shuddered. "I ask because I don't know what happened back there, and I'm worried about you."

"Oh." She felt tiny, small.

"Yeah, oh."

"Then yes, I'm fine," she whispered.

29

"Good." Instead of moving away, he slid his palm over her shoulder, along her bare arm, and then twined their fingers together. Before she could object, he had her walking beside him. And it felt… right. Even if she knew it was wrong.

Then again, she hadn't killed him, had she?

With each step toward their destination, her need for him grew. It was as if because they'd found their mate, the parts of her were willing to work together. The anger and hate she held remained vigilant in the back of her mind, while her cat snarled and paced. But regardless of their actions, their desires were exactly the same: make Wyatt Dane theirs.

Too bad for them, it wasn't going to happen. Ever.

Before long, they hit the small dirt road and found Wyatt's SUV waiting as promised. Alex's scent lingered, and the dark cloud surged, ready to defend them against another male. It coursed through her body, coating her skin and wrapping around her with an invisible barrier. It was prepared to strike, to protect.

Except… Except Wyatt rubbed his thumb over the back of her hand and with a low, murmured "easy" he had her power drifting away with a contented sigh. One touch and it was gone as if it'd never existed.

Weird.

When they reached the car, Wyatt was quick to release her hand and snare the door, pulling it wide for her. She stretched for the handle along the frame, but two large hands gripped her waist and lifted her, placing her on the seat. He didn't grunt, didn't groan or huff. Nope, it was an easy lift as if she weighed no more than a feather.

All of her liked that. The human, power, and cat all loved that she wasn't a burden or strain for him.

It meant they had a strong, powerful male.

Even if she could never have him. She had to remind herself of that. No one deserved a female who'd just as soon kill you as kiss you.

The passenger door swung shut with a low thump, and then Wyatt strode around the front of the SUV and climbed behind the wheel. The engine roared to life and then settled into a deep, rumbling purr that reminded her of a satisfied cat.

Would he purr for her like that?

No, he wouldn't, because he wouldn't get the chance.

"You're still staying at Gina's, right? With the Mastin sisters?"

Millie cleared her throat. "Right."

"Okay, then."

They didn't say anything else for the rest of the ride. Not a word as they wove through the trees, following the two lane road until they hit the more populated areas of Ridgeville. They twisted and turned their way to Gina's house. They passed other small houses, easing by even some of the larger near-mansions, and then they finally stopped outside her temporary home.

Wyatt cut the engine and silence reigned inside the vehicle. The low chirp of birds and the rumble of random cars passing came to them, but still they remained quiet. Seconds ticked past, more and more of Wyatt's scent filling the small space, and Millie's panther was going crazy. It wanted him. Period. It didn't care about that other part of them, the dangerous, deadly portion that threatened to steal control. The cat purred and whined, cajoling her to close the distance between them and rush into his arms. It'd take one kiss and then she'd be lost.

The thought clear in her mind, she snatched the door handle and yanked. She shoved it wide and hopped to the ground, intent on hiding in the house.

"Millie!"

She ignored the echoing thud of the SUV door closing, ignored the rapid thump of booted feet on concrete as he chased her. She was running like a coward, but she figured she was saving his life by remaining alone. She hadn't hurt him today, and maybe wouldn't tomorrow, but someday she'd lose control. That couldn't happen.

Millie dug in her pocket, searching for her keys. She tugged and fought the material of her shorts. Maya had assured her they were sexy and looked awesome on her ass. That also meant they were tight, and it was hell getting anything out.

"Damn it." She grumbled and yanked, tearing the keys free with a giant pull.

Normally one of the Mastin sisters would have unlocked the door for her, but they were probably hiding in their room. Men still scared the ever living hell out of them. Then again, men still scared the ever living hell out of her, too. Except for one...

Wyatt's warm hand engulfed hers, stopping her from pushing the key home and opening the door. "Don't you think we have a thing or two to discuss?"

Millie shuddered and swallowed the whimper that gathered in her throat. He wrapped around her like a delicious blanket, and she forced herself to remain still when all she wanted to do was snuggle into his arms. Her banked arousal flared to life, burning her from inside out. She ached for him, and her body yearned for his touch.

The way his breath hitched, she assumed he'd caught the scent of her arousal.

Damn it, damn it, damn it.

"I," she licked her lips, "I don't know what you're talking about."

His hold shifted, that hand sliding up her arm, along her exposed skin until he got to her shoulder. He used a gentle grip as he urged her to turn around. He was tender as he eased her to face him. The

32

action was more of a question than a rough order, so she allowed herself to be moved.

"You know that's a lie." His voice was a low, gentle baritone.

Millie shook her head. "I can't…" Tears pricked her eyes. She couldn't, but how she wished she could. Looking at Wyatt, staring into his deep blue eyes and seeing a pain so near her own, she really, really wished she could. "I just can't."

"Okay." He nodded. "I'll do the talking then, okay?" At her answering nod, he continued. "You're my mate and I'm yours, yes?"

"Yes," she whispered. The panther's joy filled her, the emotion tinged with something akin to happiness that came from the ball of her power. That alone, that change in its behavior, scared her.

"I take it you don't want to be my mate?"

Fear, hot and fast bolted along her spine. She wanted to say yes. Wanted to cry and tell him it couldn't happen, but terror kept the words inside her. Tears burned her eyes, a hint of pain so familiar now, and she blinked them back.

"I…"

Wyatt rubbed her arms, palms sliding over her exposed skin and goose bumps rose in his wake. "Shh… It's okay. Don't worry." His gaze focused on her, his eyes intent as he stared at her. "The truth is, I can't be yours, either."

Not won't, can't.

Sorrow tainted her relief at his words. They were denying each other. The cat wailed and whined while the hint of happiness her power held drifted away. It was back to being filled with anger and rage. Wetness slid over her cheek, and she realized she was crying. Tears left moist trails in their wake as they escaped her eyes.

"Aw, Millie." Wyatt brushed away one tear and then another. "Don't cry. We don't want each other. It's not right or wrong. It just is."

A lump formed in her throat, and she tore her gaze from his to stare into the distance. "I don't *not* want you. I just can't."

"So we're in the same boat." He wrapped his arms around her, tugging her forward, and she let him. "I can't have you either and it's killing me." It was true. She sensed the certainty in his sadness tainted words. "But you're better off without me."

She stood in the circle of his arms, drawing in his scent, and laid her head against his chest. She memorized the steady beat of his heart. She'd never forget it, never lose the rhythmic thump. The cat yowled, reminding her they could keep it with them forever if she'd just claim him. They would be one until the day they died.

But there was a reason he denied her just as there was a reason she denied him. She didn't know the details, but what did it matter? Knowing wouldn't change the fact she was sending him on his way.

Still crying, she eased back and stepped out of the circle of his arms. She brushed new tears from her cheeks. "Goodbye, Wyatt. I'll…" She coughed and swallowed, willing away the knot clogging her throat. "I'll do my best to avoid you. It'll hurt too much and…"

And she'd die every time she saw him.

Millie moved to face the door, but Wyatt snared her hand and kept her prisoner for another moment.

"Millie. What's your full name? Who am I walking away from?"

Why did life have to be so fucking hard?

"Amelia. Amelia Beth Walker."

"Bethy." He eased her close once again, cupping her cheek with his free hand. He urged her to tilt her head back, and she realized she could deny him nothing. "Goodbye, Bethy."

Millie opened her mouth to repeat the farewell, but the words froze in her throat because suddenly Wyatt was there. His lips ghosted across hers, teasing her with a barely-there caress. He repeated the move, brushing their mouths together in a gentle kiss. The third pass held more passion, more need that mirrored her own. He flicked her lips with his tongue, tempting her, and she succumbed to his sexual lure.

She parted her lips for him, letting him delve into her mouth. His flavors exploded across her tongue. The warm sweetness paired with darkness had her knees going weak. She clutched his shirt, depending on him to keep her upright as she lost herself in his kiss. His tongue tangled with hers, stroked and teased her with sexual promise.

Millie returned every touch, drinking in his flavors while searching out more of his taste. Her nipples pebbled and hardened while her pussy throbbed and ached. Her clit twitched, silently begging for attention, and she moaned against Wyatt's lips. He wrapped her in his arms, pulling her flush against him. Their bodies aligned from chest to knees. She felt each hard rise and gentle dip of his carved muscles, and she wondered what it'd be like to trace them with her tongue. Another jolt of need struck her with the thought.

The thick hardness of his cock was trapped between them, firm and long against her abdomen. Unable to stop herself, she rolled her hips, rubbing his length and drawing a groan from Wyatt. She repeated the caress, the move arousing both of them. Her pussy grew moist with her arousal, slicking and preparing to be filled by his dick.

She wanted him, ached for him, but… it wouldn't happen. She couldn't allow herself to become blind to the danger she posed.

Reluctantly, she pulled from the kiss, easing her mouth from his in slow increments. He growled at the first easing of pressure and moved to recapture the passion. But Millie wouldn't let that happen. Kissing him, teasing them both, was a dangerous, dangerous game. She didn't want to push her luck, didn't want to tempt and tease her power with an open target.

Placing a hand on his chest, she held him steady as she moved back and pulled her lips from his. She huffed and puffed, her breathing coming in heavy pants as she fought for control. The cat was content with the taste of their mate while her power remained cautiously pleased. Except the next push that separated their bodies enraged them both. The cat and the dark cloud read her intent, and they objected. Loudly.

She tore herself from his embrace and threw her body against the door, putting space between them.

"Bethy?" Concern laced his tone.

"No. Stay back." When he moved to step closer, she held out a hand to forestall him. "This can't happen. We said that. Both of us."

Sadness descended over his features, sadness and heartbreak. "I know." He took a step toward her, and more of his scent reached out to her. Her resolve cracked, the wall she'd built beginning to crumble. "One last touch and then we'll be done."

One last touch. She took a moment to memorize his features. The small scar that bisected his eyebrow and the nick on his cheek. The way his lips were red from their kiss and the hint of scruff that made him look dangerous. The deep, dark blue of his eyes that held a hint of gold from his lion. The closely cropped, brown hair she wanted to stroke.

She tried to remember all of it.

His fingers were callused and scratchy as they glided over her cheek, and she savored the small shudder that followed the stroke. "Goodbye."

CHAPTER *four*

"Yeah, yeah, home is where the heart is. It's also where you'll find ice cream. I'm more concerned about the ice cream than the heart." — Maya O'Connell, Prima of the Ridgeville Pride and woman who may occasionally be heartless, but she's *never* without ice cream.

After hours of pacing and fighting his lion for control, Wyatt settled on drinking himself unconscious. The cat couldn't rage at him if he wasn't awake. It couldn't scrape and claw at him if he passed out in the middle of the floor.

That's where he was when he jolted awake; spread out on his back in the middle of his living room.

At some point, the sun went down, and darkness enveloped Ridgeville. He wondered if that happened between the vodka and rum. Or was it the rum and tequila? Didn't matter, the result was the same. Bethy was at home while he was flopped on the worn carpet of his living room. Alone.

Which was how he should be, right?

A memory rushed forward—Wyatt alone at school, sitting in the principal's office while they figured out what to do with him. *"What to do with him."*

They would have sent him home with his mother, but wait, she was the one who left him there. He'd never forget the disgust in her eyes when she'd looked at him that last time.

Demon...

So much for unconditional love.

If he wasn't good enough for the woman who struggled to give birth to him, how the hell could he ever be good enough for a woman?

He couldn't.

Wyatt jumped from not-so-happy memory-land. Instinct kept his heart rate steady and breathing even, but he was alert. The lion growled in warning, on edge and wary of what roused them.

He stretched his senses, asking and getting help from the cat. He let his lips open the tiniest bit and drew air in through his mouth with his next inhale. The house's flavors slipped over his taste buds. He acknowledged his scent and tossed it aside, as were the delicate aromas from his houseplants and the mold growing on his dishes in the sink. He really needed to do some cleaning.

The soft shuffle of a foot on the carpet reached him, and he risked opening his eyes a tiny bit. Lids slitted, he searched the darkened interior of his home from his position on the floor. He didn't move any other muscles and continued to feign sleep. His mind was probably playing tricks on him, his lion pissed as hell and fucking with him, but he still needed to be careful.

Another soft scrape of displaced carpeting and then movement at the end of the couch snared his attention. He had to fight to see through the darkness of his home, but eventually he found a pair of glowing, yellow eyes focused on him. They floated midair, but his lion didn't seem too upset by the invasion of their territory. Actually, it seemed rather... pleased.

On the next inhale, Wyatt realized why. Honeysuckle and sweetness filled him, and he was equal parts overjoyed and devastated. He managed to walk away from her once for her own good. He wasn't sure he'd be able to do it again.

"Bethy," he murmured her name. The name he'd decided to give to her. Everyone called her Millie and Amelia seemed too big of a name for someone so sweet and tiny. She was all of five feet nothing with lush curves in all the right places. Sweet. Beautiful. Strong. Bethy fit her. His Bethy.

She whined and eased closer. A shaft of moonlight peeking through the curtains highlighted her, and the blackness of her fur swallowed the glow whole. She was like liquid midnight as she crept nearer, and he was in awe of her slick, lean form. His lush Bethy was a gorgeous, deadly panther.

He wanted to run with her, chase her, and pin her beneath him.

Bethy walked toward him, lessening the distance between them, and he lifted his hand while leaving his elbow against the floor. "Sweetheart."

Another whine ended with a chuff. The last feet separating them disappeared in a fluid rush as she moved to nuzzle his palm. She rubbed her muzzle over his fingers, her golden eyes hidden behind her midnight lids. She caressed him with a soft, feline sigh. She marked him over and over again, coating his hand in her scent.

Wyatt wondered if she'd do the same to his entire body.

That thought, of course, had his cock thickening and pressing against the zipper of his jeans. God, he was a sick fuck. Getting aroused while stroking his animal-shaped *mate*. But when she purred against his palm and shuffled closer, he didn't give a damn.

He sank his fingers into her thick fur and scratched her skin, smiling when her purrs increased in volume. She drew even nearer, her deadly paws nudging his side. Except he wasn't afraid, not of her, his big, purring kitten. She snuffled and scraped a sharp fang over his palm before nosing the center and encouraging him to pet the top of her head.

"I've got you." He kept his voice low. The moment seemed to call for quiet whispers.

Bethy huffed and in a flop of limbs, collapsed at his side. She went from standing to slumping against him in an instant. Her furred back pressed against his side while her head rested on his outstretched arm. She wiggled and shifted for a moment and then whined. He reached over with his free hand and stroked an ear, gentle caressing the lightly fuzzed skin. The touch drew forward a deep purr that vibrated them both.

"Is that the spot?" She chuffed in response. "Okay, then."

Wyatt rolled and aligned his front to her back. His cock had deflated with her sudden crumple to the ground, and now their position was one of comfort. He stroked her, digging his fingers into her fur.

Before long, she settled into a low, satisfied purr that soothed them both. Every once in a while, she nuzzled his arm, rubbing more of her scent on his skin. And Wyatt did the same, burying his face in the fur of her neck. She was his and his alone.

"I won't let you go, Bethy." The panther sighed and seemed to relax. "You're getting a bad deal with me—you should know that—but you're mine now. I could walk away once, but not again." He slid his arm between her forelegs and settled his palm over her chest.

His mother hadn't wanted him, had called him a no good piece of shit, a demon. He was going to hell, and he shouldn't ever taint anyone with his poison. It was all true; he wasn't worth the blood in his veins, not to a woman. Anyone deserved better than him.

"You should have better than me, but I can't let you go now."

Bethy's sigh was her only answer; the sound followed by a questioning trill. He couldn't tell her. Not then. Not right now. Not when he would be confessing to a panther and not the human half of his mate.

"Later. I promise. I'll tell you later." She responded with a soft growl. She raised her head, and yellow eyes focused on him while she flashed a hint of pure white fang. "I will. In the morning, after you're awake, I'll tell you anything you want to know."

Bethy settled once again, snuggling into him, and her scent eased him back into slumber. His mate rested in his arms, safe and content. He didn't think there was any other place he'd rather be.

The morning would be hard, gut-wrenching, and painful, but she was worth every jolt of emotional agony.

Bethy was worth everything.

* * *

Something was wrong. The thought came to him the moment he took his first wakeful breath. His eyes sprung open, and he scanned the living room. The empty living room. In a split-second, he rolled to his feet, paying no attention to the aches that accompanied a night spent sleeping on the floor in his human form. Joints popped and cracked, but he ignored the tiny hurts.

His mate was gone. Bethy had spent the night at his side; the sleek black panther snuggled against him hour after hour. Every time she sighed, he woke, quick to reassure her with a soft stroke of his palm over her fur. She quieted immediately, quickly slipping back to sleep. The ritual repeated at least a half-dozen times throughout the night, but he didn't mind. To have her so close, protected in his embrace, he'd endure anything.

But had it been a dream? Empty liquor bottles littered the room. At least two dozen decorated the furniture, and he wondered if he'd imagined her.

No. Her scent tormented him. It still coated him and permeated his clothing. He looked at the ground, noted the smudges of wet dirt and saw quite a few stray strands of midnight fur. No, it wasn't a dream. She'd been in his home.

But where was she now? He intended on working things out this morning. He didn't want to spill his guts and give her reason after reason to reject him, but it was necessary.

Instead, she vanished.

Wyatt ran a hand over his face and then rubbed his palm over his short hair, demanding his body wake the hell up and get with the program. His head pounded out an unsteady rhythm, the alcohol clouding his mind, but he didn't have time to be hungover. They'd taken a step forward last night, and he told her he wasn't letting her go.

Had she gotten cold feet?

Hell.

It didn't matter. She was his. *His*. She just needed to get that through her thick skull.

Her thick, beautiful, alluring, desirous—

Hell, he was going on and on about her damned *skull*.

He was so gone.

With a shake of his head, he padded through the house, taking note of his surroundings. He'd have to do some remodeling and a shit-ton of clean up before she came to live with him. The home was solid, but it was a bachelor's place. The interior decorating consisted of furniture he'd randomly accumulated over the years. It was all broken in and well-used. Castaways. Kinda like him.

He reached the kitchen and snatched the phone off the wall. He scrolled through the phone book and finally came across the number for Gina's house. A quick push of a button and the phone rang the home.

It took four rings before someone came on the line. Silence greeted him, but the sound of soft breathing eventually reached him. Ah, he'd heard the Mastin sisters still weren't speaking to anyone, especially men. After everything they'd endured in Alistair's clutches, he couldn't blame them.

"Hello? Is Beth— I mean, is Millie there?"

Seconds ticked past, and he wondered if the woman would answer his question. Finally, a single, whispered word came to him. "Shower."

With that, the call ended, the slam of the phone on the receiver echoing in his ear.

Okay, his mate was in the shower. Wet. Naked. Warm. Sweet.

Wyatt's cock went hard at the thought of sliding in behind her and tracing the path of every droplet of water. He didn't kid himself— there was a lot to work out—but he couldn't wait to taste her skin.

Soon.

CHAPTER *five*

"Once upon a time, I was wrong. And then I woke up and realized it was a nightmare. Whew. That was a close one. Because, really, women are never wrong. Men are just confused." — Maya O'Connell, Prima of the Ridgeville Pride and a woman who is always right and never wrong. If Alex disagrees, he can shift and spend the night with his furry ass in a cave for all she cares.

Millie stared at herself in the mirror, gazing at the bruises peppering her skin. A deep purple blotch covered her shoulder while another spanned her ribs and traveled south over her abdomen. Dirt clung to her, dark smudges along her arms and caked on her fingers. She looked at her feet and noted that it stuck to her toes.

What. The. Hell.

She turned and presented her back to the mirror. What worried her most were the twin puncture wounds on the back of her left shoulder. They were small, almost hidden by the dirt.

She reached back and ran her fingers over the wound. Small scabs flaked off with a touch, revealing pink skin. So, not that old then. But where had they come from? She'd gone to bed around ten, her body shaking with the need to hunt down Wyatt, but she'd managed to resist. The cat, even the dark cloud of her power, urged her to go to him, but she refused.

Wyatt was better off without her. There were so many things fucked up about her. She refused to burden him with her very existence.

The first of which was her tendency to strike first and question later. Except her strikes were getting stronger and stronger with every passing day. She wondered how long it'd be before she killed someone. Today? Tomorrow? Next Sunday?

Shaking her head, she turned to the shower. She'd speak with the two pride Sensitives she'd been training with, Maddy and Elise, about her night. They'd been working with her on her control as well as teaching her how to soothe and mentally interact with others.

The events of the night were missing, blurry and unclear, but it was obvious *something* happened. They could hopefully tell her what.

A quick turn of the knob and the water burst from the spigot. In seconds, it was warm and soothing against her palm as she tested the temperature, and she tugged on the dial, sending the water spraying against the tile. When she stepped under the spray, she released a soft sigh. The heat stroked her, calming her and washing away the evidence of her missing night. Brown, dirt-filled liquid slipped from her body, revealing her pale skin. She snared the soap and sudsed a washcloth. In moments, she was scrubbing her skin and exposing even more of herself. A few new bruises came to light... Including several on her thighs. Very near her inner thighs.

Had she been...?

Her cat snarled in objection, the animal rushing forward for the first time since she'd awoken. No, the panther would know.

Wouldn't it?

She hoped so.

Ignoring those swaths of darkened flesh, she resumed washing herself. She scoured her body, with jerky, efficient movements until she was squeaky clean. It took no time to wash her hair, lathering up the strands in seconds.

Millie stepped beneath the spray and let the full heat of the water rain on her. She sighed as it seeped into her bones and relaxed her. So good. So hot.

"Hmm…" she hummed.

"That sounds delicious." The deep baritone echoed in the room, bouncing off the tile walls and pinging against her nerves.

A scream burst past her lips before she could stop it. In the back of her mind, she recognized the owner of the voice, but that didn't stop her from reacting. Immediately the ball of rage responded to her fear as the panther rushed forward, ready to protect her. The feelings of both parts of her converging at once had her falling to her knees. She couldn't hold herself up, not when the two of them worked together.

And, oh God, she was going to kill him—they were going to kill him—all before she had a chance to regret sending him away.

Millie waited for the screams, the yells, or roars that always accompanied what she gifted on people. When she killed Alistair's man, even when she'd knocked out Harding all those months ago, it'd been lightning-fast. Now, with strength came a longer, harsher attack; one that could last minutes instead of less than a second.

Instead… instead, he grunted and nothing more. Just a quick, low sound followed by… silence. There was no falling and the telltale thump of his body colliding with the tiled floor. Nope. A grunt.

Millie eased toward the edge of the shower curtain and reached for it with a shaking, trembling hand. Before she could stop herself, she slid the plastic back enough to peek into the small bathroom.

There he stood, larger than life and more gorgeous than ever. A rough scruff covered his cheeks and chin, attesting to the fact he hadn't shaved. His clothes were wrinkled, and his shirt creased as if he'd slept in it. The same went for his jeans.

"Wyatt?" She didn't care that her voice quaked.

He grunted again. "That bitch of yours packs a mean punch, huh?"

Millie's power bristled at being called a bitch, but settled at the compliment. "Um, yes?" She tightened her grip on the curtain. "Not to be rude, but what are you doing here? In the bathroom. In Gina's house."

He furrowed his brow in confusion. "You left me and I promised we'd talk. Besides, this is where you are. I told you last night I wasn't letting you go. You stayed. So here I am."

The words were matter-of-fact. As if nothing was odd about his statements. Except she hadn't seen him last night. They'd parted ways at her front door, and she spent the rest of the evening wishing she was strong enough to bend her power to her will.

There was no way.

But what about the bruises? The scrapes and mud and dirt? Did I somehow… No.

"I don't know what you're talking about. Can you—can you leave? Please?" Her fingertips ached, and she pretended the cat wasn't coming out to play, imagined it wasn't trying to take control. She was nervous, worried, almost scared, but she didn't need her panther. She didn't know much, but she knew her mate wouldn't hurt her. At least, she didn't think so.

"Last night," he furrowed his brow. "Last night, in my living room. You stayed the night and then disappeared."

Millie shook her head. "No, I stayed in my room last night. I didn't leave."

Liar. What about the mud?

48

"Bethy—"

Her gums ached, fangs growing and pushing aside her teeth. "Please. If you won't," she cleared her throat and kicked at the panther. "Can you let me finish my shower? Please."

"Okay, sweetheart. But I'm not leaving the house. I know you were with me last night. I *know* it."

Sweetheart.

The word niggled at her memory. There for an instant, then forgotten and swept away to the back of her mind.

"We can talk about it when I'm done."

Wyatt nodded. "Okay. I'll be waiting."

She wasn't sure if it was a threat or a promise. And she wasn't sure how she wanted to take it.

The moment the bathroom door clicked shut, finalizing his departure, Millie turned off the shower and stepped out. She snared a towel and dried with quick, efficient movements. She ignored the twinges of pain and aches that made themselves known. Each shift of muscle sent another pang through her.

Something happened last night.

Wyatt seemed to believe she'd spent the evening with him.

If she had, did he cause her bruises?

No. She didn't know how she knew, but she did.

So… where?

With a shake of her head, she pushed the worry from her mind. She'd talk to Wyatt, and together they'd figure out what happened. Because, no matter what, she'd gone through hell and been bitten by

49

something last night. It sure as fuck wasn't a lion. She glanced at the two pink dots on her back. No, definitely not a lion.

Millie slipped on her shorts, sans panties, hissing when they slid over her hips. Her bra was quick to follow and was just as quickly discarded. No way. Not with the darkening bruise on her ribs that seemed to wrap around her and ended below her armpit. It wasn't happening. Instead, she tossed on her loose T-shirt and called it good. She'd be flapping in the breeze, but it was better than being in pain.

Taking a deep breath, she opened the bathroom door and stepped into the hallway. Wyatt's scent was concentrated there, as if he'd stood there and lingered before entering. Or he stuck around after he'd left, listening to her moan and groan as she dressed. Neither prospect was appealing.

The deep sound of Wyatt's voice reached her, and she instinctively felt the urge to go to him and sink into his embrace. The cat was annoyed with his sudden appearance, but it also recognized safety. Why couldn't the little shit make up its mind already? First happy, then pissed, then happy and now satisfied.

Millie strode down the hallway, ignoring the twinge in her left foot. She was led into the living room by the voices, freezing when she emerged into the open space and found... Alex. The Prime. Oh, God, not now. She was already fucked from her lost night and Wyatt's presence and now...

Her body reacted to the male. That's what he was. Simply a man invading their territory. He threatened them. He could hurt them, and she couldn't let that happen. The billowing anger rose, the cat hot on its heels, and she spun, anxious to run and save Alex any pain.

Her body waged war on itself. Fight or flight. The power and her cat wanted to fight. Fight hard. Fight deadly.

Two strong arms wrapped around her, sheltered her, protected her. With the unexpected touch, the urge to do battle receded. It flowed to the back of her mind and curled up in a satisfied, calm ball. One meeting of skin and skin and he had her calming.

"Wyatt," she sighed and slumped into his arms.

"I've got you, Bethy."

He held her, the two of them breathing in sync as her body drained of every hint of rage. Muscles she hadn't realized were tense eased and relaxed into his embrace until she was a boneless mass.

Wyatt nuzzled her neck, and she tilted her head to the side, granting him more access. Even if she couldn't have him, she wanted him. He was a drug she ached to be addicted to for all time. He lapped and licked her skin, tongue gliding over her moist flesh. Then a sharp fang scraped her and she shuddered at the seductive caress.

"I'll always have you, Bethy." He whispered the words against her skin and then blew a warm puff of air over her. "Always."

The sound of a throat clearing popped their seductive bubble and Millie stiffened in Wyatt's embrace.

He was quick to tighten his hold for a brief moment. "Tell that part of you to quit being a brat. The cat too." He nipped her shoulder. "Now."

And those parts listened. Traitors.

Wyatt eased his hold, hands sliding along her arms before cupping her shoulders and turning her to face him. A sexy grin graced his mouth, and she fought the urge to kiss him, capture his lips and slide her tongue into him.

One kiss hadn't been enough.

Another throat clearing had her narrowing her eyes while he rolled his own.

"C'mon. Alex needs to talk to us about yesterday."

"Last night?" She couldn't imagine he'd spoken with the Prime about last night already.

"The picnic." He released her shoulder and stroked the bridge of her nose. "Last night is between you and me."

"Oh."

"C'mon." Wyatt tugged her forward and deeper into the living room. He settled her on the couch and immediately took up the space beside her, snuggling close and practically encircling her with his presence.

Millie clutched his hand, nerves wreaking havoc on her body. Her cat and power stirred, but Wyatt's touch soothed her.

"So, Millie," Alex began, and she wanted to correct him. She was beginning to think of herself as Bethy. Wyatt's Bethy. "Why don't you tell me why I'm still standing? Maya thought a child would keep you from lashing out, but now… "

She stared at the Prime, knowing he wanted an answer she didn't want to give. Things were… complicated to say the least. Was she keeping Wyatt? He seemed to think so. Even the cat and her power were on board with that plan. But part of her knew he deserved more than a broken woman who couldn't interact with anyone without his touch. And what if that trick stopped working? What if she grew too strong to be cowed by Wyatt's dominance? What if—

What if, what if, what if…

Millie closed her eyes and licked her lips, knowing she was about to commit herself to a man who deserved so much more than she could give.

"Wyatt is my mate." His hand tightened on hers, squeezing gently, and she sensed his rising happiness at her statement. God, she prayed it wasn't a mistake. "He's able to keep things steady."

"I don't sense," Alex raised her eyebrows. "A *completion* of your mating. What I do sense is pain." His nostrils flared. "A lot of it."

*

Wyatt breathed deep and followed the scents coming from his mate. His mate. She'd said the words aloud, to the Prime no less, and now he wouldn't allow her to take them back.

He let the air in his lungs out slowly and then drew in more, hunting for what Alex had discovered and… there. It was there. Hidden beneath the strawberries and cream of her shampoo and the light floral aroma of her soap. Pain. So much damned pain.

"Bethy?"

She tensed and looked away. He placed a fingertip below her chin and urged her to return her attention to him. The cat was going ballistic, sensing her aches weren't emotional, but physical. It railed at him that they hadn't sensed it sooner. It was pissed they'd left her alone in the bathroom when her body was hurt.

Bethy allowed him to move her, and he sucked in a breath at the agony that filled her gaze. "What happened, sweetheart? You were fine when we fell asleep. You didn't say anything earlier."

Tears filled her eyes. He hated that each time he saw her, she sniffled and cried. "I don't know. I don't remember. Until you said something about last night, I thought I slept here. Wyatt, I—"

He grasped her hand and pulled her closer, tugging until she rested against him. "Hush." He rubbed her back and then froze at her wince. "I've got you."

He met Alex's gaze over her head and noted the man's concerned frown. "Is she—"

"We'll be fine. Can we finish this later? Lemme figure out what happened?" Tears soaked his shirt, and the cat panicked, pushing forward in an attempt to protect their mate from whatever caused her distress. His gums ached, and the tips of his fingers throbbed with the impending appearance. "I'll call you later, Prime. I need to care for my mate now."

The Prime opened his mouth as if to object, but Bethy shifted her attention, head turning toward Alex. Whatever the man saw, it caused him to snap his lips together. "I'll wait for your call."

In moments, the front door opened and then clicked shut once again, signaling the Prime's departure.

Rather than rush Bethy into an explanation, he simply held her. He enjoyed her solid weight against his chest, reveled in the way her curves molded against him. His cat purred in delight. Now that the presumed threat from Alex was gone, they could relax. Especially since the scent of their mate's pain dissipated with every breath.

That didn't mean he was about to forget it, though.

"Bethy?"

She nuzzled his chest. "Hmm?"

"We need to talk."

Bethy huffed and slumped against him. "Do I need to move? Wyatt, it's so comfortable here. Doesn't hurt."

"Aw, sweetheart," he murmured against the top of her head. "Why don't you tell me what happened last night and then I'll give you my version."

She buried her face in his shirt, and when she spoke, her words were muffled by his clothing. "I went to bed around ten and woke up around eight this morning. That's what happened."

Wyatt shook his head. "No, you came by my place around eleven in your panther form. Your cat is sleek and gorgeous, sweetheart. You're like liquid midnight. Crept up on me, and I didn't even know

54

you were there until you were nearly on top of me. You meant to alert me, didn't you?"

He had no doubt she could have pounced and slit his throat before he even realized she'd entered his home. Panthers in the wild were sneaky.

"No," she shook her head and pushed away from him, wincing as she shifted position. "I slept. I woke." She shuddered and gripped the bottom of her shirt. "I woke up with these," she whispered as she lifted her top to expose her bare stomach.

The pale, plump skin was covered in varying shades of purple.

"What the hell? You fell asleep beside me." He reached out to touch her skin, but froze when she jerked back. *Damn it.* He had to remember that her saying the words didn't automatically mean she was ready to move on to the next step. "You were fine when you laid down. You marked me with your scent and then we curled up on the living room floor."

"I don't—" She shook her head.

"Yes. You stayed shifted, and we formed our own human-kitty pile. I swear it, Bethy." He needed her to believe him. He hadn't done this. He hadn't hurt her.

She must have recognized his worry. "I know you didn't hurt me. It wasn't you." She let her shirt fall to cover her once again. "But are you sure it was me?"

Vulnerability filled every part of her and Wyatt was quick to soothe her. He grabbed her hand and cradled it between his. "We may not be fully mated, but you are mine, sweetheart. I have your scent. My cat won't ever forget it. So when I say you were beside me last night, I assure you, it was you and not some other panther. *You.*"

"I don't remember." She closed her eyes and turned her head away. "I woke up covered in mud and bruises this morning. And a bite on my shoulder."

The lion surged, tearing through him like a damned runaway car and shoving itself forward. In a blink, fingers became claws, skin became fur, and his human mouth reshaped to his cat's muzzle.

Something, someone, had bitten *his*.

Rage thumped and pushed at him, sending adrenaline through his entire body and shooting his anger rocketing through the sky.

His.

But then… Calm. Soothing, cool, calm enveloped him. It was as if a soft kiss was pressed against his soul while a gentle hand stroked his uncontrolled beast.

A small hand rubbed his chest, fingers sliding over his thin shirt and tentatively caressing him. "Easy. I'm… Well, I'm not fine, but I'm okay."

Wyatt breathed deep and drew her, all of her, into his lungs. He identified every ache by scent, noted the worry and fear that coated her skin, and then there was this *other* that mingled with the aromas.

The other had to be the bite.

Another stroke of her palm over his body and he willed the cat back. They'd figure out what happened, discover who dared to hurt their mate.

Because one thing was for certain: Bethy had been attacked, beaten and *bitten* somewhere between his home and Gina's. And she didn't remember a moment.

The question became: why? And better yet: who?

"Shh…" Her voice was soft, lyrical, and he realized she was using her power on him, lulling his cat into submission.

"Bethy, do you realize what you're doing?" From all accounts, she had been having more than a little problem with control. Hell, she herself was surprised he hadn't been fried to a crisp.

His mate froze and snatched her hand away from him. "I-I calmed you." Panic tainted the air. "How did I calm you? I can't do that. I can't go into someone's head and calm their beast. My power bludgeons people, not soothes them. They keep trying to teach me, but it doesn't… I can't—"

"Easy. My turn to calm you. I'm fine. I'm not going to hurt you, and the cat is under control. Easy." He tugged her back to him. "Do you have bruises anywhere else? I need to see the bite." He couldn't help the lion's growl in his voice. "And don't try to pet that anger away. I'm allowed to be mad when another puts his *fangs* in you."

Bethy chuckled. "God, are we going to spend the rest of our lives telling each other to chill out?"

Wyatt smiled and rested his cheek atop her head. "If we're lucky." He rubbed her hair, transferring his scent to her. "But no changing the subject." She sighed, and he ignored it. "I need to see what was done to you and then we can figure out what we're going to do next. It scares the hell out of me that you were hurt, and even more that you don't remember anything about last night."

He eased away from her and pushed to his feet before holding out a hand for her. He waited for her to grasp it, to have a little faith in him. "You trusted me to hold you through the night, Bethy. Trust me to take care of you now."

CHAPTER *SIX*

"The perfect mate can give you the big O with a single touch. He can make you feel sexy, delicious, and totally kick ass. No, wait, that's ice cream. Never mind." — Maya O'Connell, Prima of the Ridgeville Pride and woman who is cheating on her mate with ice cream. Currently, the ice cream is winning.

Millie trembled the moment their palms touched. Funny, she hadn't been nervous in his embrace, but now... Now she was going to expose herself to him. Physically, at least. Emotionally... Someday. He knew some of what she endured, what she was capable of, but he didn't know about the dark parts of her.

Problems with control?

Right.

Taking a deep breath, she gripped his hand and allowed him to draw her from the couch.

"In your room?" His voice was low, soothing.

She thought about going into her bedroom and stripping down, exposing herself to him amongst dirty sheets and in a space filled with her daily anguish. No.

"Can we..." She licked her lips and fought for courage. Supposedly she'd gone to his home. She could go there again. She had a future with Wyatt. She needed to begin thinking as a mate and a mate would want to be in his den. "Can we go to your place? Maybe being there will remind me about last night."

The blooming smile at her question fell, and she cursed herself. She should have quit while she was ahead. Jarring her memory wasn't the only reason to go to his home. She opened her mouth to tell him that, but he'd already stepped back.

"Sure. Go grab what you need, sweetheart." The words were right. The tone was not.

"Should I," she paused, wondering if she was going to give voice to the question in her mind. The panther and her power urged her to say the words, but the human half of her still worried over the next steps. "Should I bring things for," she closed her eyes and got the rest of her question out in a rush. "Should I bring things for overnight? More than one night?"

Quiet. Nothing. He didn't respond, and God she was such a fucking idiot. She should have kept her mouth shut, should have been happy with an afternoon, but *no* she had to ask—

"I would love any time you would give me, Bethy. An hour, a day, forever. Whatever makes you comfortable."

Millie gulped and forced her eyes open. The emotion in his gaze struck her, dug through her battered body and dove into her heart. For the first time in her life, her panther, her power, and her human self were on the same page.

"Give me a few minutes to pack and leave a note for the Mastins. They'll come out after we leave." She didn't wait for him to respond and instead dashed off. She had to run and get packed before her nerves failed her.

Her room was still a mess, the blanket and sheets caked in mud while deep furrows marred the mattress. At some point, she'd shredded her blankets and dug right through to the springs. She avoided

60

looking any deeper, unwilling to face what'd happened. Then again, she didn't know what had occurred. What she did know was all three parts of her didn't want to remember.

And that scared the hell out of her.

In quick, efficient movements, she packed a duffel bag with a few changes of clothes, including a nightshirt. Knowing Wyatt was her mate and giving herself to him were two entirely different things. She wanted to be covered as she slept.

Millie tossed the bag on a chair and strode toward the bathroom, intent on grabbing some of her toiletries. She was *not* going anywhere without a toothbrush. Halfway to the bathroom, a pale piece of something caught her eye. It was pristine, pale cream even though it sat atop a ribbon of dried mud.

Padding toward the object, she bent down and picked it up. It was paper thin, light and airy and no bigger than a quarter. Huh. Something niggled her mind, poked and prodded at her, but refused to be jarred loose. Flashes of remembered pain and tears, agony and hopelessness along with the desire to just… die.

Damn it. It was there, just beyond her reach.

She kept hold of the small piece of something, and went into the bathroom. She wrapped it in tissue and decided she'd tuck it in her bag. Later she'd show it to Wyatt and get his opinion.

For now, she had to get through the ride to Wyatt's.

Taking a deep breath, she let it out slowly and finished gathering her belongings. In minutes, she was ready to go and striding into the living room.

Her mate stood near the front window, his back to her as he stared into the street. He was so strong, so solid and fit and powerful. He was everything she'd always dreamed of having in a mate. It wasn't just his body that drew her. It was the innate goodness she sensed in him.

Now she needed to make sure she was worthy of such a male.

"I'm ready."

Wyatt turned his head toward her, and she met his amber gaze. The lion inside him was still very near the surface, and she didn't think it'd retreat anytime soon. Especially once it caught sight of her bruises and the bite on her shoulder. She had to admit it worried her, much more than a little.

"Then let's go, sweetheart." He closed the distance between them and took the bag from her hand. "I won't be able to rest easy until I've got you in my den and can look over your injuries myself."

Inside she knew he wouldn't hurt her like those in her past. He would care for her. She had to trust him. He was her mate, her one, and everything inside her demanded she put her faith in Wyatt.

So, she would.

Millie followed Wyatt out of the house and to his SUV. Once again, he lifted her into the seat, and she fought to hide the wince that came with the action. "You're beat up more than just your ribs, huh?"

The words were tender; the tone was not.

"I'll be fine."

"Uh-huh."

She forced herself to sound more confident than she was. "Really. I'm sure my panther will fix me right up."

Even though it hadn't yet, which scared the hell out of her even more.

"Uh-huh." He pushed her door closed and then moved around the truck to climb behind the steering wheel. "We'll be home in a couple of minutes."

We.

Home.

Something inside her, the barrier she'd kept between them, cracked and pieces crumbled with the words.

"Okay. I don't... I don't remember last night, so it'll be good to see where you live." Panic assaulted her at the loss of memory once again.

"I know, sweetheart." He reached over and snared her hand, twining their fingers. "We'll figure it out."

Millie didn't say a word after that, content to bask in his confidence. He believed his words whole heartedly, so she would believe in him.

Fifteen minutes later, after leaving the center of Ridgeville and traveling down a two lane road, they pulled up before a nice sized ranch-style home. A garage occupied one end while the rest of the house was spread out to the right.

A flash, a snapshot, burst from her memory, and she realized she'd seen this before. She climbed from the SUV before Wyatt could come around and help her. She shoved at the door and ignored the blooming ache in her ribs as she stumbled to the ground. The red door. The blue shutters. The far right window with a broken latch.

She lurched forward, sandal-clad feet skidding on the gravel driveway, but she kept moving toward the house.

"Bethy!" Wyatt wrapped an arm around her waist, and she hid the wince that came when he brushed against one of her larger bruises. She leaned against him, but refused to let him slow her.

"I remember your house."

When he tried to steer her toward the front door, she wouldn't be redirected. She kept moving, traveling to that broken window. There was no way she could know all of this unless she'd been there.

"Bethy, sweetheart."

"One second." She broke from his grip and pushed past the low bushes. "My paw prints." She pointed at the ground. She'd seen her own often enough to recognize them as hers and hers alone. "My nose." Smeared wet spots had dried on the glass overnight. Testing her own memory, she tugged on the window, and it rose without a sound. "She was determined. She must have let go enough for me to get it open for her."

"I didn't even realize it was broken." He paused and looked at her, brow furrowed in confusion. "She?"

"My panther." She tipped her head toward the now open window. "Sneaky bitch."

"You talk about her as if you two aren't the same." He frowned. "I know we talk about our cats, our animals, as something separate. Sometimes we act more animalistic, but you're saying—"

Millie looked away and shrugged one shoulder. He had to know eventually. "Think of it as split personalities. There's me. There's her. Then there's the other." She swallowed against the growing lump in her throat. "We're not like everyone else. We're all different. Different voices. Different personalities. Just… different. Dangerous."

He pulled her into his embrace and she let him. "You're perfect and don't let anyone tell you differently. Dangerous? Only to anyone who threatens you."

Millie snorted. "You mean everyone."

Wyatt shook his head, but didn't say anything. "C'mon. I'll fix the lock on the window real quick. I need you safe. Then we'll take a look at that bite and those bruises."

She didn't mention she could take care of herself. The hate-filled part of her ensured her protection.

Millie looked at the ground, noting the disturbed dirt and the other odd pattern in the soil.

Or did the power fail to keep her safe?

*

"C'mon, sweetheart." Wyatt urged her away from the window and toward the front door. Before he stripped his mate bare, he'd take care of the broken window and double check the others, as well as the back door. He had no doubt there were quite a few other scrapes and bruises marring her pale skin. Plus, he imagined there was more to her story than a lost night.

He was determined to find out.

At the front door, he was quick to unlock and push it open, holding it wide for his mate. His lion chuffed and rumbled in pleasure the very moment she stepped across the threshold and entered their den. They had her now, safe and in their home, and they wouldn't let her go. He'd been secretly pleased she'd been willing to come to his home. He wanted her within his den. Thankfully, she'd given him an easy way to accomplish that feat.

Once inside, he pushed the door shut and made sure the locks were enabled. He'd have to add another one or five. He needed to ensure Bethy was safeguarded.

Wyatt flicked the light switch and illuminated the interior of his home, wincing as light spilled across the living room. Crap, his house was a disaster area. It hadn't seemed so bad when he woke, but he'd also been half asleep.

The furniture looked more worn than he remembered, and there might be a half-dozen or so empty bottles of beer on the end table. Plus the empty liquor bottles. And then there were the pizza boxes on the coffee table, and he was pretty sure there were a couple of slices in there. He'd decided to save them for later.

He winced. Yeah, he wasn't the cleanest lion in the pride. At all.

"Um, here." He rushed around her and grabbed a couple of the empty bottles, pausing to brush off one of the couch cushions on his way. "Go ahead and sit down and I'll…" *Make a wish that the house was fucking clean.*

A soft, delicate hand on his arm had him stilling. "Wyatt, it's fine." She shook her head, and the sight of her gentle curls bouncing had his cock going hard.

He was the sickest. Fuck. Ever.

He got turned on by his injured mate's *hair.*

He'd never tell a soul.

Well, unless the other guys admitted it first.

"I'm sorry. I wasn't expecting to bring you back here. I mean, you were here last night, but you were a panther, and it was dark."

Bethy scrunched her nose, and he wanted to kiss the tip.

He was pussy whipped without the pussy.

"I think I remember the house." She shook her head. "I know I recognized the outside, but in here. The scent…" She sighed. "Maybe I'm just tired."

Wyatt looked at her with a critical eye. Purple bags lingered beneath her eyes and lines of fatigue marred her face. He reached out and brushed a lock of hair from her forehead. "You slept well beside me, but we don't know what happened later."

66

"I know I was here." Her eyes were filled with so much hope, and he knew his sweet Bethy was torn up about not remembering. "I mean, I've never been here before, but I remember the house and the window and the scent inside your home."

"It's a good start, sweetheart." He grabbed her bag from her hand and then snared her fingers in his loose grip. "Let me show you the guest room. I can assure myself, and my cat, you're okay and then you can lie down."

Wyatt wasn't going to mention she hadn't been up long, and it worried the hell out of him that she wanted to nap already.

"Guest room?" She pulled against him, snaring his full attention.

"It's that or my room, sweetheart." He laid it out there and would let her decide.

"We're mates, though."

"Yeah." He wasn't going to let hope bloom.

"So we belong together. I can't promise..." A blush tinged her cheeks, and she waved her hand around. "*That*. But can I sleep in your bed?"

"Sweetheart, you can sleep wherever you want." He squeezed her fingers gently and let his lion's purr travel through him.

"Then take me to your room." A tremble traveled through her fingers and into him, but he decided to take her words at face value. They both had their demons, and it was hard and nerve wracking as hell to deal with them.

"Okay, then." He resumed his slow, but steady steps.

Wyatt led her down the hallway, thankful there weren't dirty clothes littering the ground. In his bedroom, he sent up another prayer of thanks he hadn't left the space a complete disaster area. Sure, there were a few random bits of clothing—thank God, no dirty boxers—but there were no empty bottles or half-eaten pizzas hanging around.

He looked toward the pile of his discarded sports gear. A lot of the men in the pride tended to get together for anything from basketball to hockey and anything in between. Everything needed to play any of those sports was carelessly piled in one corner of the room. Dirty or clean—mostly muddy and dirty—were stored there. He really should have rinsed his cleats after that last game at the park. He looked at the bat lying on the ground, caked in mud after he'd tossed it away to tackle Harding. Okay, cleats and bat.

Once inside, he released her and stepped aside, letting her take a good look around the space. "We can swap some of this out if you'd like. I'm not attached to any of it. It's just stuff, and I want you to be happy, Bethy."

She was silent as she looked around and then finally turned to him, flashing him a bright smile. "It's you, Wyatt." She shrugged. "And that's all I need." Taking a deep breath, she walked to the bed and stroked the comforter. "Will you help me? My muscles are bunched, and the bite is on the back of my shoulder."

Skin. He was going to touch and stroke her skin. His cat was still furious she'd been hurt, but a tiny part of him looked forward to caressing her.

"Sure." His voice was husky, the growl of his cat imbuing the single syllable.

Wyatt dropped her bag, not caring where it landed or if it struck anything. He only had eyes for Bethy.

In two strides, he was behind her, his hands hovering over her shoulders. His cock, his wayward fucking cock, twitched and half-filled. "How do you want me to help you?"

"Just," she held her breath and he did the same. Would she change her mind? "Just grab the bottom of my shirt and help me work my arms out."

"Then off?" He was torn between wanting her to say yes and not wanting to rush her into anything she wasn't prepared for.

"Not-not yet."

"Okay, sweetheart, whatever you want." He did as she asked, grasping the bottom hem of her T-shirt and gently lifting it.

Her pale skin was revealed in minute increments so he wouldn't accidentally harm her further. The first inch or two pleased the cat, the animal purring at the idea of their mate being exposed to them. But it was the third inch that had his beast ending its purr and rolling it into a low growl.

Purple bathed her skin, starting above her hip bone and traveling along her back. The more revealed, the more bruising he found. Some spots were pale blue, while others were dark purple, attesting to the depth of the injury.

A barely perceptible shudder wracked Bethy's body, and he cut off his growl, cursing himself for scaring her. "Sorry, sweetheart. I'm not mad at you. Just mad you're hurt."

"I know." He sensed the conviction in her softly spoken words.

He paused as he neared her shoulders, holding the fabric as she wiggled and shifted until her arms pulled free of her shirt. It was then he realized she wasn't wearing a bra.

Holy hell, she was trying to kill him. Even in the face of her injuries, his cock went from slightly stiff to rock hard. If he moved and peered over her shoulder, he could catch a glimpse of her bare breasts. He imagined them full and round, nipples practically begging for his mouth.

Damn.

It took a few more tugs and shifts, but finally her arms were free of the fabric and he was able to expose her shoulders. More bruising, what looked like a boot covering her left shoulder. And on the right... Thin twin puncture marks. Too far apart for any of the small shifters they had in the area. Not nearly separated enough for it to be one of the lions in the pride.

He let her tug the shirt from his grasp and cover her chest with the fabric as she hugged herself. He was sad to lose the chance at seeing her body, even if it was bruised to hell and back, but he was more worried about the bite.

He gently brushed his hand over the wound, noting the skin was slightly warmer around the holes when compared to the rest of her body. Yet, there was no redness or sign it was infected or irritated. In fact, all he really saw were two small injuries that were slowly healing.

"I know you're beginning to remember coming to the house. You can't think of where these came from?" He kept his voice low, knowing his sweet mate was probably nearing the end of her rope.

Bethy shook her head. "No. I went to bed and woke up covered in mud, scratches, bruises, and that."

He raised his eyebrows. "Mud?" He took another look at her back, seeing evidence of the scratches she mentioned. "When did you get out of bed this morning?"

"Eight. You showed up around eight-thirty."

Wyatt glanced at the alarm clock's glowing red numbers. "We're at just after nine. These scratches should have healed by now. Definitely some of these bruises. And this bite is still very pink."

Bethy swallowed; throat working and the desperate half of him wanted to lick a line along her neck. "I know. I don't know why it's not." Another tremble, but this one was accompanied by a wave of anxiety.

The lion forced him to move, demanded they gather her close and comfort her. Then again, Wyatt didn't even try to resist his instincts. He immediately gently pressed his front to her exposed back and wrapped his arms around her waist. He worried she'd rebuff him, shove him away, but instead she sighed and gave him her weight.

"We'll figure it out together, sweetheart. You mentioned you're not together like other shifters. It might be a matter of your cat or your power getting you into trouble." She shook her head, and he nuzzled her neck, drawing her scent into his lungs. "Yes. But no matter what it is, nothing is going to happen to you. Do you understand? You're mine, and I'm going to take care of you even if it means tying you to my bed."

Wyatt winced. Damn, talking about tying up a woman who'd spent years being abused by Alistair was the most insensitive thing to say. Ever. "Bethy, I'm sorr—"

She spun in his arms, turning to face him, and he met her golden gaze. Hints of darkness lingered in the golden orbs. He wondered if that was the third part of her, the power she referred to as something separate from the woman and cat.

"Don't be sorry. You…" She shook her head and turned her focus to his chest. "You haven't treated me like I'm broken."

Wyatt shrugged. "You're not."

"But even after you found out I could hurt you, you didn't treat me differently."

He raised his eyebrows. "But you haven't hurt me. Everyone is so afraid of you, Bethy. Everyone is so worried about you hurting them. Maybe the part of you that's angry is taking care of them before *they* could hurt *you*." He cupped her cheek and forced her to tilt her head back. "And maybe that part of you that lashes out at everyone else doesn't touch me because it knows I'd die to protect you."

Wyatt waited, hoping she sensed the sincerity in his words. Because he meant them. Every. Single. One.

Minutes ticked past, and she didn't say anything, didn't move, breathe or blink, and he wondered if he should apologize. He wasn't sure why he'd be apologizing, but Alex had told him that when it came to mates: apologize first, figure out why later.

"Bethy—" He didn't get the words out. Not when she pressed to her tiptoes and brushed her plump lips over his. Not when she lapped at his mouth, and he opened for her. Not when she slipped her tongue into his mouth and drew him into heaven.

*

Millie sank into him, letting him take her weight as they kissed. She was so damned tired, bone hurt, and needed to lean on someone— on him—for a while. The women in the pride had been wonderful to her, but Wyatt was… hers.

His tongue tangled with hers, dancing to a seductive beat while they kissed. His warmth filled her, sinking into her body, soothing the remaining aches and pains.

Her cat wanted him, her power desired him, and her body couldn't live without him. She'd tried so damned hard to push him away, but she realized now there was no way they wouldn't be together. They fit. Period.

Wyatt wrapped his arms around her waist, and she let him draw her closer until their bodies were aligned. His hard muscles pressed against her curved body, and she wondered for a moment if she was enough for him. Then she realized his thick cock wasn't hard for anyone else. It was all her. She had him desperate and needy. She had him growling and purring at the same time.

He stroked her back, hands sliding along her spine and then settling on the curve of her ass. His fingers flexed and gently cupped her roundness, kneading her with infinite care.

He pulled his lips from hers and rested his forehead against her. "Damn, Bethy, sweetheart. Make me hurt." She wrapped her arms around his neck, stroking the smooth skin, and he purred. "Make me want." She jerked forward and nipped his lower lip, smiling with the small shudder that shot through him. "But we need to stop." His grip shifted from pulling her close to nudging her away. "You're hurt and I'll be damned if I'm some horny asshole—"

Millie rubbed her nose against his while tightening her hold. "No, don't." She tilted her head and leaned forward, nuzzling his neck. "You're— This is the first time— I can't promise I'm ready for a lot, I've never just touched or enjoyed or lov— It's always been—"

Millie huffed. God, she was fucking things up two hundred million ways from Sunday. And she sure as hell hadn't been about to say "love." She didn't know him well enough. At all. The cat could act on instinct and her power was just bizarre. But her human half knew sharing a couple of kisses and spending a couple of hours together wasn't enough to jump from "nice to meet you" to "I love you more than chocolate cake."

"Whatever you want, Bethy." His voice was hoarse as she licked his neck, savoring the salty flavors of his skin. She wanted to follow every line with her tongue. "I'll give you anything."

She knew he meant the words, sensed the truth and conviction behind them, but that didn't mean jumping into action came easily. She nibbled his flesh while she figured out her next move. She teased and tempted him while satisfying the cat's need to taste and discover their mate.

The hands on the top of her ass traveled lower, cupping her full globes and squeezing them. He pressed them together, and the move transferred to her pussy, teasing her lower lips. Her heat clenched and she instinctively rocked against Wyatt's hips, drawing a deep moan from him.

"Sweetheart, we need to stop or lay down because my legs won't hold me much longer." The sexual promise in his voice had her easing away from him. It had her sliding her hands along his arms and finally catching his wrist before he could move away.

Her clothes were still more off than on, but she didn't care. He knew what she looked like dressed, and he wasn't turned off by her curves. She flicked a glance at the bulge in his jeans. No, he wasn't turned off at all.

"Come lay with me, Wyatt." She tugged as she stepped back, closer to the bed. "I don't think I can—"

"I'll thank God for whatever you will give me, sweetheart."

She nodded, accepting his statement at face value, and let herself sit on the edge of the mattress. Which put her at eye level with a certain part of him. Fear hit her in a quick spike, but her cat shoved the feeling down. It hadn't trusted any other male—ever—but it wanted and needed Wyatt. It wasn't about to let the human part of her ruin things.

Taking a deep breath, she released him and wiggled backward onto the bed. She made sure her top stayed draped across her breasts as she shifted and slid until she sat in the middle. Wyatt still lingered near the edge.

"Bethy…" Doubt lingered in his voice, and she held her hand out for him.

"Come lay with me. Kiss me. Touch me. I'll do the same to you and we'll go from there." A heated blush filled her face. "Just don't expect everything."

An emotion she didn't want to examine filled his gaze. "Anything is everything to me."

"Then come here." It was as if he was waiting on the added reassurance. Because suddenly he was there, and stretched out beside her. He was still dressed in his shirt and jeans, but the fabric molded to his muscled body, outlining every chiseled part of him.

74

Now that she had him where she wanted him, what the hell should she do?

Her shirt brushed her bare breast, reminding her once again of its presence. Taking a deep breath, she grasped the material and lifted it from her body, sliding it over her head in a rush and then tossing it away.

She squirmed, worried at his reaction. The bruises still stained her pale skin, but then she caught the pure heat in his eyes.

"Damn." He reached for her, hand pausing when his palm was inches from her right breast. "Bethy?"

She reached out and cupped the back of his hand and guided him toward her body. "Touch me, Wyatt. I'll tell you if something's wrong, but I need you to touch me. I need my mate."

It was like a switch flipped because then he was there, easing her to lie against the mattress, his large body spread out beside her as he propped himself on an elbow. As if waiting for her to bolt, he slowly brought his hand to her breast, obviously still worried she'd panic.

"Wyatt, love me like you'd love any other woman," her panther snarled at the idea that another had touched him. "I promise to tell you if I'm scared. I said that already."

"But—"

"I'm gonna bite your ass if you don't stop treating me like I'm made of glass."

Wyatt grinned. "Promise."

She really was ready to bite him, but then he gave her what she desired. He cupped her breast, hand holding the fullness while his thumb flicked her nipple. "Oh, God."

He released a low, cocky chuckle, and she promised she'd growl at him about it later. Like, after he was done scraping his nail over the

75

hardened nub. Yeah, she'd say something when it stopped feeling so good.

Then, when he captured the tiny bit of flesh between thumb and forefinger and gently squeezed, she realized it'd never stop feeling good. Especially when he locked his gaze with hers and slowly lowered his head, mouth open. He caught her nipple with his lips and plucked the nubbin before tapping it with his tongue.

The touch went straight to her pussy, yanking a moan from her chest and she arched into his caress.

"Yes," she hissed, unable to do much else.

He did it again, adding a hint of suction as he teased her, toyed with her breast and increased her arousal. Her pussy was hot and aching, growing slicker by the breath.

"Wyatt," she whined, unsure of what she wanted. Her body craved more. More of his hands. More of his mouth. Just more.

He released her nipple with a soft pop and blew warm air on the bit of flesh. "Shh… I've got you." He lifted her breast to his mouth and circled her nipple with his tongue. "Is this what you want?"

She whimpered and nodded.

"How about more? Just a little?"

Millie's pussy clenched, her body liking the idea of "more" a whole lot. She nodded again.

Instead of immediately giving her what she desired, he transferred his attentions to her other breast, treating it to the same, delicious attentions. A tap, a nibble, a hint of suction. She arched and writhed against him, ignoring the lingering aches from her deep bruises. There was no amount of pain that could banish the pleasure she derived from his touch.

Wyatt teased and tormented, her body responding to every caress, her cunt tightening and silently demanding to be filled and stretched by him. But... she wasn't there yet. Not quite.

"Wyatt," she moaned when he sucked hard. "Please."

The hand cupping her breast drifted over her abdomen, gently gliding over her bruised skin in a barely-there touch. He kept moving, stroking her, until his fingers met the button on her shorts. He released her nipple long enough to voice his question.

"Bethy?" He tweaked the button.

"Yes." *Please.*

That was all the assurance he needed. The button snapped with a quick tug and the sound of her zipper lowering warred with their soft panting. Cool air bathed the curve of her belly, and she remembered panties had been another "clothing optional" thing as well. The fact the garment was missing was driven home by Wyatt's deep moan.

"God, sweetheart. What you do to me."

She didn't have a chance to respond, not when those warm, callused fingers stroked her sensitive skin and played with the curls guarding her mound.

Wyatt leaned down and lapped at her nipple, his digits still toying with those curls. "I'm going to taste you here, sweetheart. First, I'm going to slide my fingers over your clit and then I'm going to slip two into your pussy."

She whimpered and shifted, body unable to remain still with his sexual promise.

One digit teased the top of her slit, tormenting her with the gentle caress. He was so close to where she needed him. Tilting her hips, she tried to force him where she desired and merely got a deep chuckle from him in response.

"You didn't answer me, sweetheart." He suckled her breast.

"You didn't ask a," Wyatt slipped his finger between her lower lips and brushed her clit. "Oh, God, there."

Another laugh, but she didn't care. Not when he rubbed the little bundle of "fuck yeah, more" nerves.

"Here?" He did it again, circling instead of sliding over her clit.

"Yeah."

He tapped. "Right here."

"Yes," she hissed and rolled her hips. Nothing had ever felt so good. Ever.

Wyatt retreated back to the top of her slit. "Not here."

She snarled at him; the panther's fangs dropping and filling her mouth.

He licked her nipple and grinned. "Obviously not."

"Wyatt, *please.*"

"Shh…" He lifted his head from her breasts and stretched to brush his lips across hers. "I'll give you what you want."

Millie whimpered into his kiss, deepening it when he would have pulled away. She needed his mouth, that extra connection between them as he toyed with her pussy. She tangled her tongue with his, mimicking what would eventually happen. She wasn't sure if that was today, now, but she had no doubt she'd give herself to him.

Wyatt went back to pleasuring her pussy, fingertip slipping over her clit and touching the perfect bundle of nerves that gave her so much bliss. He circled the nubbin, 'round and 'round and 'round, and she rocked with each movement.

Millie panted and moaned against his lips, pulling away enough to beg for more. "Yes, please."

He slid his touch south, slipping through her abundant cream, and she spread her legs wider. Her shorts constricted her movements, but the restriction added to her growing ecstasy. He had to fight to give her what she wanted.

Oh, yes.

He tugged and shoved at her shorts, but didn't pause to remove them. Instead, he made room for himself as his large hand moved to cup her mound. The finger that'd been toying with her heat slipped inside her, stroking her inner walls while the heel of his hand pressed against her clit.

Millie raised her hands and clutched his shoulders, fingers tightening and squeezing him. She moaned into his mouth, and he swallowed the sound as he growled in return.

He pumped his finger in and out of her sheath, caressing long dormant nerves, bringing them back to life. His tempo was slow, torturous, and maddening, but she wouldn't have changed it for the world. Because it was so very, very delicious.

"Like that, Bethy?"

"Uh-huh." She rocked against his hand, and her hip rubbed his hardness, pulling a moan from him this time.

Millie slipped a leg between his and hooked the back of his knee, drawing him closer until the heat of his cloth-covered cock burned her. Yes, that was what she wanted. She could take pleasure from him while giving a little of her own.

Now they writhed in earnest, bodies moving in a tempo only they could hear. When he pressed deep, she moaned, when his fingers disappeared she whined, but when two speared her, she screamed and sank her claws into his flesh.

"Yes!"

"Fuck, Bethy." He panted along with her, their hips moving on their own.

His digits fucked her, and she imagined it was his cock, his long, hot length spreading her cunt and pushing deep into her body. He'd hover above her, work himself in and out of her soaked sheath, and she'd love every moment. She melded their lips together as they half-fucked. Clothes separated them, but that was all that kept them from completing the act. And her fear. But fear had no place in the pleasure she experienced.

Wyatt pressed deeper, ground harder against her clit, and she hissed against his lips. "Like that?"

"Don't stop." She rolled her hips, ensuring she rubbed his throbbing dick. She knew he needed, knew he deserved her touch, and she'd give him everything.

After she came.

"Feel good? Do you like my fingers in your pussy?" The words were growled, dark and wicked.

Who the hell knew she liked dirty talk?

"Yes. Love it." She pulled him closer until he lay half atop her body, his heavy weight pressing her into the mattress. "More."

Now she could truly grind against his cock and his hand, pretend to fuck him as he sent her pleasure rising higher.

Wyatt's pressure and pace increased, plunging deeper, pushing harder, moving faster. And she loved it. Each movement had her shuddering, body reacting to his touch.

Bruises? What bruises?

All she had now was a cloud of boiling pleasure that seemed to grow and heat with every passing moment. His shirt scratched against her nipples, his tongue tangled with hers while his hand did wicked, delicious things to her pussy.

Now she was nothing more than a bubble of desire and need, the joy of release gathering close. Their bodies moved as one, each shift of muscle translating to snippets of bliss and impending ecstasy. She wanted it, needed it, and desperately ached to come on his hand.

"Please." She didn't know what she was asking for, had no idea what she needed, but Wyatt did.

His rhythm didn't falter as he kissed his way down her neck and buried his face against her shoulder. "You need to come for me, Bethy. Lemme feel it. Are you imagining my cock? I'd fill you so good. Fuck you so hard."

Yes, that's what she imagined: him inside her, tormenting her and driving her higher. Her body rushed to the edge, prepared to leap and let the gathering pleasure run free inside her. Her pussy clenched around his fingers in a joyful rhythm, milking his digits as she fought for release.

"Yes." She bucked. "Wyatt. Close."

Then he gave her what she needed. He scraped a single, sharp fang along her neck, sending a tingle of pain down her spine. The tiny hurt burst the bubble of pleasure inside her, and she came apart in his arms. She screamed with the release, rapture filling every inch of her body in a blinding rush. Her muscles twitched and spasmed, jerking as heaven crawled along every nerve. Her body was no longer her own. No, it was controlled by the pleasure he caused.

Millie's cat reacted to the bliss their mate caused, rushing forward with a blazing speed that surprised her. Black fur sprang from her pores while her teeth extended and pierced her bottom lip.

Then, like so many times before, it stole control from her. While her body remained lost in the throes of her orgasm, the cat struck. It took one great heave of muscle and then her fangs pierced flesh and blood filled her mouth. The cat luxuriated in the coppery tang as the liquid flowed over her taste buds while the human half of her raged at the animal.

Wyatt trembled and stilled beside her, body tense as she drank and swallowed drop after drop. Millie pulled and yanked at the cat, fighting with everything inside her. She beat at the animal, screamed while it bound Wyatt to them.

It wasn't supposed to work this way. It was supposed to be beautiful and glorious. Not some twisted, one-sided claiming.

Mentally she dug her fingers into the cat's fur, squeezing its flesh, and heaved as hard as she could. That did it. That one had her teeth releasing him and claws retracting. Her fur snapped beneath her skin until she was human once again.

She swallowed the last droplets of Wyatt's blood, mentally slapping her cat when it purred. "Oh, God, Wyatt. I'm so sorry." Once again, she was near tears, the moisture gathering as she stared at the ragged wound she'd inflicted. "I'm so, so sorry."

With a sob, she fled, scrambling over the side of the bed and bolting for the door. She didn't deserve him. She couldn't claim him. She had no control, pieces of her scattered, and a mind so torn she couldn't even remember the night before.

A nearby door was ajar, and she dashed through the portal. A bathroom. She could hide in the bathroom.

She darted into the space, absently gripping the wood panel and shoving it toward the jam. She waited for the resounding thud when it finally slammed closed. Except the sound she heard was actually a slap.

Oh shit. She spun around and continued her scramble backwards, fear pushing into her when she realized Wyatt had followed her.

He was here—in the room—covered in his own blood.

And she had nowhere to hide.

*

Wyatt had just experienced the most explosive, bone-shaking orgasm of his life. His cat roared in satisfaction, fur standing on end as he puffed it out in pride. The animal strutted through his mind, elated that Bethy claimed them. Yes, they still needed to claim her, but they were willing to wait until she was ready.

The only hitch came from the fact she'd fled the moment her teeth slipped from his flesh. Then he'd lost the feel of her silken skin beneath his palms and the warm press of her curved body against his.

The cold invaded him the moment they lost touch while shock held him immobile for a split second. He watched her roll from him, scramble over the covers and burst from the bed. She'd run, blindly dashing across the floor until she turned toward the bathroom. It wasn't until he saw her cross the threshold that he erupted into motion, following hot on her heels.

And what he found broke his heart.

Bethy huddled in the corner, his blood staining her mouth, neck and chest. That didn't bother him, shifter sex could be a bloody business. It was the stark fear in her gaze that worried him. She had her knees drawn up, arms crossed over her shins, and trembles wracked her balled form.

"Sorry. Sorry. Sorry. Sorry." She repeated the word over and over again in an anguished whisper.

"Bethy." He approached slowly, uncaring of the throbbing wound on his shoulder and the cooling wet spot on his jeans. Both of them were a testament to her, to their mating.

Wyatt dropped to his knees, his heart shattering at the anguish in her gaze. Doing his best to look non-threatening, he crawled toward her. Inch by inch, he eased forward, closing the distance between them until he knelt before her.

"I'm sorry." Her tormented gaze met his. "I didn't mean to. Please don't hurt me." She shook her head. "I would never have done that to you, but she's so strong."

"Sweetheart." He reached for her, giving her plenty of time to voice an objection. When she didn't say a word, he slid his palms along her arms, noting the sudden coolness of her skin. "C'mere."

He shifted his position, sitting beside her on the floor while also lifting her into his lap. He cuddled her, rubbing her exposed skin while he enjoyed having her close. With each stroke, more of the tension in her body eased until she leaned against him, trusting him with her weight.

"I'm sorry," another whispered apology.

"There's no reason to be sorry."

"I claimed you without permission. I didn't ask. I just…" She sniffled, and it broke his heart. "*I bit you.*"

"Do you know what I've wanted since I was five years old?" He would get the words out. For her, he could do anything.

Bethy shook her head, and Wyatt took a deep, calming breath. The lion knew what was coming, but that didn't keep the animal from being overcome with sadness. It whined, begging him not to revisit the past, but Wyatt persevered.

With a trembling hand, he stroked her hair, letting the repetitive action soothe him.

"My mother is human and my father is a lion. They met during a Gaian Moon and had sex, but she didn't know he was a shifter."

Bethy sucked in a breath.

He could understand her surprise. The last thing any shifter did was fuck during a Gaian Moon and not tell the woman about their animal or the chance of a shifter child.

The Gaian Moon was a time when shifters were driven to mate, to procreate and further their kind. Most sexual encounters on the night of the Gaian Moon resulted in pregnancy. Shifter women were more fertile while a shifter male's cum was more potent. Everything in their bodies was in overdrive as they were overcome by the moon.

Wyatt continued. "After they spent the night together, he disappeared, leaving her pregnant with me."

He paused, dreading the coming pain.

"We did okay. My father was just gone and my mom's parents didn't want anything to do with us, but my mother held two jobs and took care of me." The cat dug in its nails, fighting to keep Wyatt silent. Bethy needed to know how much her bite meant to him.

"Children shift…" Bethy murmured.

"Children shift as soon as they can walk. Providing they're taught how. I wasn't, but when I was five we moved a few towns over to Stratton, and she enrolled me in kindergarten." Wyatt grinned at the memories. "I made my first shifter friend…"

Memories took over for him then, he relived the events as he bared his soul to Millie.

Wyatt sat on the low wall that surrounded the playground, heels bouncing against the bricks while all the other kids played. He hated being the new kid. No one in the class talked to him. They glared at him. Whispered real low so he couldn't hear. And he could hear *really, really* well.

The other kids laughed. Some of them pointed at him.

Stupid heads.

He looked around the big space and spotted the worst of the kids. Max. He acted like he owned everything. So Wyatt glared at him and Max glared back and they just kept glaring at each other.

Something in him told him to look away, but Max was the meanie.

But then, holy cow, then his eyes got all yellow. Max ran across the playground and all the kids got out of his way. He was coming right for Wyatt!

Darn, darn, darn. He wanted to say damn like his mom, but she'd told him it was a bad word.

He crawled off the wall and looked for a teacher, scared that Max really was gonna hurt him. Except Miss Walker was just watching the other kid run at him and she wasn't stopping him and…

Max was in front of him, but his eyes really, really were yellow and there was gray stuff all over his face.

Something inside Wyatt yelled and it sounded like a cat hissing and then Wyatt had *yellow* hair on his arms.

"We don't want a cat in our town," Max growled at him.

A cat? What was Max talking about?

"I'm not…" Wyatt stuttered and stared at his hands. His fingers were *black*.

The other boy pushed him and he noticed that Max's fingers were black, too.

"Miss Walker!" Wyatt didn't get much more out because then Max was hitting him and it hurt and he hit back and…

86

Bethy shifted his hold, reminding him he still held his mate. With his free hand, he rubbed the small scar that bisected his eyebrow. "Max tore into me." Wyatt's cat chuffed at the memory, the first time they'd connected. "There's fur and claws and I've got no idea what's going on, but then something in me comes to life."

"Your lion." She nuzzled his chest.

"My lion. It tore through me so fast." He shuddered at the remembered pain. "I didn't have any training, didn't know about shifters, and then I was one."

He quieted for a moment, gathering the courage to finish his story. His lion whined, nudging and pulling him away from the memories, but she needed reassurance, and he needed to give her his trust.

"Max and I got into it, but he's an Alpha. Even then, he was the strongest on the playground. A new shifter doesn't have much of a chance against a wolf pup who's destined to rule a pack." He grinned, remembering the scratches and scrapes. "I held my own though and when the teachers finally separated us, we got hauled into the principal's office."

This was where his story took a dark turn, but he pushed on.

The school's main office was stuffy. Stank like Missus Carmichael's old lady perfume and nasty towels when his mom left them in the washer too long. Blech.

Wyatt picked at the wood on his chair, feet swinging and banging against the legs while he and Max waited to see Mister Simons.

"Do you think we're in lotsa trouble?" He whispered to Max and the boy shook his head.

"No, my dad's the Alpha. He'll tell Mister Simons to leave us alone."

"What's an Alpha?"

Max groaned. "Don't you know anything about shifters?"

87

Wyatt shook his head. "I didn't know until I did this."

He held up his left hand. It was still covered in yellow fur and his fingers were long nails.

The office lady, Missus Laurens, glared at him. "Wyatt Dane, put those claws away right this second. This is a no claw school, young man."

He shook his hand. "But I dunno how."

"I'll tells him Missus Laurens." Max puffed out his chest. "Whatcha gotta do is…"

Wyatt was happy Max was helping him with his hand. It kept him from thinking about his mom coming to get him.

She was gonna be so *mad*. He always did good in school, though. So maybe she wouldn't be super mad. Maybe a little mad.

Max kept talking about a cat and a wolf and some sorta animal.

He hadn't ever been in trouble before. His mom always told him he was her bestest boy. He hoped he still would be when she finally showed up.

"Are you listening?" Max pushed him.

Wyatt snarled. He opened his mouth and showed his teeth to the other boy.

"Wow." Max pushed at his lips. "You gots big teeth. I bet you're a lion. Missus Laurens, do you think Wyatt's a lion? I bet he's a lion. Why are you going to school in Stratton and not in Ridgeville? Ridgeville's the lion town and we're the wolf town and—"

"Enough, Max." Missus Laurens interrupted his new friend. "Finish teaching him how to shift back. His mother is human, so he doesn't know."

Max looked at Wyatt, a frown on his face. "I'm sorry your mom is human. That's so sad."

Bethy rubbed her cheek on his chest, reminding him he wasn't five years old anymore.

"I was scared as hell, but I thought it was so cool. I sat in the office staring at my hand, trying to figure out how to get my claws back. Max and I spent an hour together where he taught me how to partially shift. How to talk to my cat." He dropped a kiss to the top of her head and let his lips rest there as he drew in Bethy's scent. The flavors of their sex still lingered, and he inhaled them. "I had my fangs out and one hand shifted when my mother walked in."

The click of her high heels reached Wyatt first. He knew that sound, how his mom walked. He was super scared, but super excited too. She'd be really mad, but look at the cool things he could do now.

"I wanna do my teeth and one hand," he whispered to Max.

Max rolled his eyes and sighed. "Then tell your cat you need his help to do teeth and one paw. You gotsa talk to it."

His mom was getting closer. *Click clack, click clack.* Wyatt closed his eyes and went looking for his lion. It was still puny and small, but Max told him it'd get bigger when Wyatt got bigger. So that was okay.

He thought about what he wanted to look like and showed it to his animal. The lion made happy sounds and then he felt the tingle in his hand and his teeth hurt a little bit. But it was okay if it hurt because it was really cool when it was done.

By the time his mom came in the room, he was all shifted, and he waved to her, making sure she could see his cool new claws.

"Hi, Mommy!" He shook his hand harder. She needed to see how awesome it was. He opened his mouth wide and showed her his teeth, too.

He wanted to bounce in his chair, but Missus Laurens already yelled at him and Max about that. So he didn't.

But... but Mommy didn't smile.

Well, that was okay. She was super mad because she had to leave work and come and get him. She'd be happy about it later.

Except, she wasn't frowning at him anymore. She was... Well, her eyes were real, real wide and her mouth was open and she was real white. Something burned his nose, the stench hurting him from inside out.

"Max, what's that?" He'd been smelling things more and more since Max started teaching him about his lion.

"Fear. She's afraid of something."

"Mommy? I can take care of you if you're afraid." Wyatt kicked away from the chair and jumped to the ground. "I'm a lion now, and I—"

His mom held her hand out. "Stay back!"

More of that icky scent hit him. "But I can make you not afraid. Missus Laurens, tell her about my lion and—"

"Sit down, Wyatt!" the office lady yelled at him and he listened.

Max told him that even if he was a lion and stronger than other wolves, he still had to listen to grownups.

Then Missus Laurens grabbed his mommy and took her into Mister Simons's office.

"*What have you done to my son?*" his mom screeched and he couldn't hear what Mister Simons said. "*A what?*"

"Didn't your mom know about your lion?" Max whispered to him.

"No," he answered back and then was quiet. He wanted to hear what was going on in the principal's office.

"A shifter…"

"No, he is *not* whatever that is. He's a boy. You people at this school did something to him. What did you do?" His mom was really, really afraid and that made him afraid.

The thing inside him whined and scratched.

Mister Simons talked some more, but Wyatt couldn't hear what he said.

"No, he's not one of those *things*. I don't care what you say."

"Now, Miss Dane…"

"I did not give birth to *that*." His mom was hissing like Wyatt's lion. "Where is my *son*?" He was right here. Right on the chair and waiting for her. "I did not give birth to *that*."

Wyatt's eyes hurt. Like he was gonna cry. But big boys didn't cry unless they were bleeding and he wasn't so… He sniffled and wiped his nose on his sleeve.

"Why don't you sit and I'll explain, Miss Dane." Mister Simons sounded nice. Like he was trying to help.

"I've heard of you people. Of you *things*. I've heard whispers in town." Wyatt had never heard his mom that mad before.

"We're regular people like everyone else, ma'am."

"No. You're not. You're a bunch of demons and that… *demon* out there is just like you."

His eyes hurt some more and his cheeks were wet, but he wasn't crying. His mom was just mad about him getting in a fight. She didn't really mean those things. She couldn't. He was her bestest boy and sometimes he did bad things, but she said she'd never stop loving him. That's what moms did. They loved their kids.

"Look, his father was a piece of shit and left me and now I find out that *thing* is no better?" His mom stomped across Mister Simons's office and the door knob jiggled. "If he's so special, you keep him. I don't want him, and I doubt anyone ever will."

The door swung wide, then his mom stepped out. She stomped toward the other door, the one that led to the hallway, and she didn't look at him. Her face was all red, but she wasn't crying. No, his mom was super mad.

"Mom?" Wyatt hopped from the chair and stepped toward her. "Mom, I'm really sorry for fighting." She stopped and looked at him. She still looked upset, so he smiled. His mom couldn't ever stay mad when he smiled.

Except that made her madder. "This is what his father was? On the inside?"

Mister Simons answered her. "Yes, Miss Dane. I'd like you to perhaps take some time—"

"No," Wyatt's mom glared at him. "If I would have known, I would have aborted him."

"Mom…" What was she saying? He stepped toward her, holding out his hand. She always held his hand when they walked. She didn't want to lose him ever. He was her bestest boy.

But Mom… Mom scooted back and then she was in the hallway and she was running and…

"Mom? Mommy?" He didn't know what aborted meant, but she was his mom and she was leaving. Mister Simons reached out for him, but he was faster. He ran past the principal and into the hallway, yelling after his mother. "Mom, wait. I'm sorry! I won't do it again!" She got to the door that led to the parking lot and flung it open. The sun lit up the hallway and then it slammed closed behind her. "Mom!"

Large hands grabbed him, stopping him, but his mom was leaving without him. She was supposed to pick him up. "I'm sorry, Mom!"

His eyes hurt really bad now and his cheeks were all wet and he didn't care if Max saw him cry because his mom left him and said he was a demon, but he wasn't. He was a good boy. He was!

"Mom!"

Bethy's small hand sliding over his chest pulled him from the painful, horrifying memory. "Wyatt?"

Wyatt wiped away the tears on his cheeks. Damn it, every time he let the memories come through, they made him fucking cry.

He took a deep, shaky breath. "It took my mother an hour to go from loving me to loathing me. Sixty minutes." He'd remember that last look for the rest of his life. "Bethy, my own mother didn't love me. She was disgusted by me. Hated me for what I am. Told them I was a piece of shit like my father and simply gave me away without a second glance." He tightened his hold, the old pain surging inside him once again. "Gave me away like I was nothing. Mister Simons didn't explain abortion to me then. It took years to finally realize what she'd meant."

Wyatt voiced the same question he'd asked himself over and over again throughout the years. Every time he got close to a woman, every time he was tempted to enjoy himself on the night of a Gaian Moon, he voiced the question.

"How can I be a mate or a father, when I couldn't even be a son?"

Bethy's full weight slumped against him as if she deflated and then she moved, changing position until she straddled his lap. Small hands cupped his cheeks, and he allowed her to move his head.

"Wyatt, I don't ever want you to think that again. Ever." He noted the single tear trail its way down her cheek. "You," she sniffled. "God, you don't even know." She shook her head. "Even when I told you I was dangerous, you didn't care. You just wanted to be with me. Even when I sent you away, you came back."

He eased her hands from his face and stroked her cheeks, catching the next tear that fell. "To be fair, you came back first."

She sniffled. "Shaddup. The point is, any other man would have walked away. Hell, most of the pride won't come within a hundred feet of me. I only got to go to the picnic because Maya promised everyone they'd be safe. And you chased me down…"

"I didn't know you could kill me," he countered.

This time she growled and his cock twitched in his jeans. Hell, he came a handful of minutes ago, and he was ready to go again.

Bethy glared at him, and her fangs grew to peek past her upper lip. In a lightning fast move, his hands went from wiping away her tears to pressed against the wall beside his head, her grip holding him captive. "Stop it. You're mine. You'll always be mine. If I fucking say you're the best fucking mate, you'll listen. Your mother was a bitch—period—and you are so much better than her sorry ass."

"Sweetheart," he grunted because then a set of white fangs flashed before sinking into his uninjured shoulder. She bit down, and the scent of his blood permeated the room in an instant. His dick hardened fully, coming to attention with the feel of his half-nude mate pressed against him, her fangs in his flesh.

As quickly as she struck, she released him and sat back. She ran her tongue over her lips, gathering his blood, and moaning when she swallowed it down. "Mine."

It hurt, but Wyatt nodded with a smile. "Yours."

She leaned forward and licked the wound before laying her cheek on his shoulder. "You deserve more than a mate with a deadly case of split personalities, but no matter what, Wyatt Dane, you deserve to be loved." She sighed. "I promise to do my very best to finish getting there."

Finish getting there...

Wyatt couldn't doubt her conviction, couldn't doubt the feelings behind her words. He just wasn't ready to believe in himself. He tested her hold, pressing against her grip the tiniest bit and he lowered his arms when she released him. He rested his palms on her hips, stroking the exposed skin and dipping beneath the waistline. The button was still undone, zipper still lowered, which gave him room to touch her. He noted the fullness of her ass, the way it filled his hands. He peeked over her shoulder and stared down at the top curve of the globes. He wanted to nibble and taste her there. Well, everywhere.

He also noticed something else, something he could hardly believe.

Bethy didn't have a single bruise, not even a hint of green or pale blue indicating her injuries were still healing. They were gone. "How do you feel, sweetheart?"

She glared at him. "We're not talking about me. We're talking about you and not believing—"

Wyatt grinned at her frown. "I'm asking because you're not bruised anymore."

"I—" She snapped her mouth shut and looked down at herself, squeaking when she seemed to realize she was half naked and bloody as hell. Her small hands jerked to cover her abundant breasts. And didn't do a very good job of it.

It didn't keep her from looking though. She wiggled and squirmed, forcing his cock to throb and ache with need while she pulled and pushed her breasts this way, and that to look at her stomach.

"They're gone. How the hell…" She looked over her shoulder, neck muscles straining with the move. "Is the bite…"

Wyatt abandoned his spot at her hips and slid his palms along her sides, tracing the curved lines of her body. "Lean forward."

Bethy did as asked and pressed her front against his chest more fully, giving him a perfect view of the back of her shoulder. Regret, anger, and pain hit him from all sides while the lion released a monumental roar.

"I'm sorry, love. It's still there."

CHAPTER *seven*

"Love your enemies. It pisses them off. Then again, I prefer stabbing them with whatever's handy. But you know, potato, potahto." — Maya O'Connell, Prima of the Ridgeville Pride and woman who doesn't give a damn how you say potato, she's still gonna throw it at the bad guy.

The rest of the day had been quiet, easy. Wyatt hadn't put any other pressures on her, and she'd done her best to quietly apologize for tearing into him like he was a porterhouse. They'd both had a lot to think about. He with his past and hopefully realizing she was bound and determined to love him, while she…

Millie reached across and rubbed her left hand over the two small scars on her right shoulder.

They'd decided that maybe the cat had been holding back because it'd wanted Millie to mate. As soon as she'd tied them together, the panther jumped into the game and took care of healing her. Unfortunately, that hadn't stretched to the bite on her shoulder.

She let her fingers worry the small, raised bumps, fingernails scraping against the sensitive skin as she fought to remember how she'd gotten them. Still, her mind came up blank. Snippets of her night spent with Wyatt began returning—his blood seeming to jump-start her memory—but there was nothing between the time she'd left Wyatt and the moment she woke muddy and bruised.

She stroked the scars again.

Why did they feel so familiar? The cat urged her to leave it alone, to stick close to Wyatt and stay inside. Scarily, her powers agreed.

Millie growled at herself, snatched her hand away and spun from the window. What did they know? They couldn't be bothered to be part of her instead of separate beings.

She shoved aside their desire to forget, to shield her from the memories. She stilled, turning inward and digging through the shadows of her mind. Her Sensitive abilities darted left to block her while the cat crouched low, ready to pounce. It didn't matter, she would have her way. The events of the previous night were just out of reach, so close yet still outside her grasp.

Inside herself, she stepped forward only to be brought up short by the cat. She bolted left and was halted by the cloud of rage. Another move to the right and it swirled around her, enclosing her in the darkness.

No. She would know, damn it.

Millie pushed and struck out at the ethereal ball, swinging her arms through the darkness. Fuck.

Taking a deep breath, she did the one thing it wouldn't expect. She'd always been careful, cautious, and afraid. Screw it. She'd never know anything if she didn't fight for it. She crouched low in her mind, gathered her strength, and jumped head first into the cloud. She dove through her thoughts, flew past the cat and rage alike and deeper into her own mind.

It seemed like hours later she collided with the ground inside her, slid across the smooth surface and finally slowed and stopped. She felt the cat and her power tear at her, roar and pull on her in objection.

It didn't matter. She'd gotten what she wanted. The past lay open before her, ready to be brought forward.

Except last night. Somehow she'd slipped beyond the prior evening and deeper into herself.

Unlike what she'd been told by Maddy and Elise, her mind was not like a massive room filled with filing cabinets just waiting to be opened. They'd told her over and over again that their thoughts and experiences had to be kept orderly, that her brain would automatically keep things organized for her. A Sensitive couldn't function and use their powers properly without some sort of order.

Millie took stock of her surroundings and realized that part of her problem stemmed from her cat and ability's constant battle to hide things from her.

Her memories weren't ready for her in small stacks, but were scattered like sheets in the wind. Each page contained yet another remembrance, but they were random and messy.

Though, the most recent events were slightly more orderly. She moved beyond them, past her months in Ridgeville, assaulting Harding. Then, even further along through the time she'd been hidden away in the compound.

From there... Oh, dear God, from there...

Bits and pieces of her life were strewn through the darkness. Would she ever find herself amongst the mess she faced?

Millie paused near a small pile of memories and reached for them with a trembling hand. Panic assaulted her, her cat and that cloud of rage forcing their emotions on her. She paused, fingers a hairsbreadth from those sheets of paper. Did she want to know? The other two parts of her were fighting her, pummeling her, trying their best to keep her from looking into the past.

She didn't care.

Millie let her fingers wrap around one sheet, tips gliding over the memory in a trembling caress and then she was thrown into that piece of her past. Was she eleven? Twelve? No, thirteen. Yes, thirteen and locked in a well-known room. The space was a memory the other parts of her had allowed her to keep. The plain brick walls with a single, solid steel door.

The lock clicked and the door slid aside to expose her visitors.

Alistair.

Alistair entered first, his midnight hair and pale skin were familiar. As were the ice blue eyes that focused on her. They glowed in the harsh light of the room, piercing her with their intensity. She feared him, yes. He beat her, attacked her, backhanded her when she talked back.

Oh yes, he scared her.

A movement behind him drew her attention and Millie froze. This was the person of her nightmares. Her heart raced, pummeling her with the desire to burst from her chest. She had to run, had to hide. Claws formed at her fingertips, the cat rushing forward. She could scratch him, claw him. But she tried that every time. Every time she attempted to injure him and every time she failed.

The male who truly terrified her stepped forward, moved into the light. He smiled at her, that wicked, deadly smile, and flicked out his forked tongue. "Hello, Millie-love. I've missed you."

"F-f-f-f…" She couldn't get his name out.

In the present, the cat and her power rushed her then, tearing her from the past and shoving her away from tortured memories. The page representing that grotesque encounter slipped from her hand, yet the feel of her own blood sliding over her fingertips remained.

She'd bled so, so much that day.

Millie fought for breath and stumbled back, catching herself on the wall. Dear God. Now she understood why those two parts of her demanded she forget. Now that she knew just a tiny hint of what her body could take, she wished she'd forget again.

Shaking her head, she fought to clear her mind of the panic coursing through her veins.

One thing was for certain, they needed to work together, not against her as they had in the past. Not knowing could be dangerous. She knew it was the cat who'd rushed things with Wyatt. If he hadn't been happy with the half-mating, it wasn't the cat who'd pay the price. It would have been the human part of her.

She knew the human body could take a lot of damage, but she doubted she would have come out the other side if Wyatt had been furious with her. Angering him, hurting him, would have crushed her.

Millie tilted her head to the side, listening for Wyatt, and heard him talking on the phone with Alex. Just because she needed him, they needed each other, life in the pride couldn't stop. She knew that.

Until he could hold her close, comfort her, she'd let the outdoor air soothe her frayed nerves.

Moving through the home, she headed toward the back, pointing at the deck as she passed Wyatt's office so he knew where she'd be. He nodded and gave her a wink with a mouthed, "be careful."

She'd always be careful, she had him to come back to.

On her way out the door, the bright pink cell phone on the counter rang. The Prima had given it to her when she'd come to live in Ridgeville and demanded she carry it always. The monstrosity buzzed and hopped along the smooth surface, and she scooped it up on the way outside. From what Wyatt said, Maya had been upset about the picnic. Millie wondered if Alex told his mate about how she'd awakened that morning. Then again, Wyatt was probably giving the Prime the details now.

It didn't matter. Millie could tell Maya herself. Stepping onto the back deck, she nudged the door closed behind her and took a deep breath. The air was clean and fresh; the scents of the city's cars not reaching this far into the country. From what Wyatt told her, the pride house was just over the next hill. Close, but not too close, he'd said.

The vibrating phone in her hand repeated the annoying ring, and she answered the call.

"Hello."

"Fi-na-lly. God. You'd think you had a social life or something." The last few words were mumbled, and she imagined the Prima speaking around an ever-present spoonful of ice cream. "Anyway. Did you get dirty?"

"Dirty?" Millie hardly ever understood the Prima.

"Yeah. Dirrty. Two Rs. Like Christina Aguilera."

"I have no idea what you're talking about." She shook her head and half-grinned as she sat on one of the deck chairs.

Maya gasped. "You don't know? It's a travesty! The world is coming to an end!" The Prima groaned and then a high-pitched squee reached her. Millie pictured the Prima bouncing in her seat. "I know! How are you feeling? Still have the need to kill people? Because I'm thinking of a smaller get-together complete with alcoholic beverages and copious amounts of dance music. We'll make sure that Wyatt holds your hand the whole time since he seems to be one of the anti-batshit people like my kidlets are. We can catch you up on what you've missed these past thirty years or so. Alex," the Prima screamed, "can we have another *par-teeee?*"

She was pretty sure she heard Alex's roaring "no" through the phone and echoing across the expanse separating the homes.

In less than a second, Maya was back, and she heard the smile in the woman's voice. "Alex said yes."

Millie rolled her eyes and shook her head. "That's great, Prima."

She snorted. "Prima-shmima. Call me Maya. I only use the title when it gets me something I want. Such as Carly's last container of Choccy Mint ice cream. Then it is awesome being mated to Alex."

That drew a laugh from her, and she smiled wide. When was the last time she'd just... laughed?

Movement out of the corner of her eye snagged Millie's attention. She turned her head, still grinning as Maya chattered in her ear about the best places to visit "downtown."

A snake slithered over the smooth wooden deck, its gaze trained on her as if she were its target. It crept closer and closer, and Millie pushed to her feet, then climbed atop the chair. Fear crawled down her spine and pumped through her veins.

Yes, she was a panther. Deadly. Dangerous. But for some reason her human mind was on the same page as both her power and her cat.

Run.

Far. Fast. Forever.

Run.

F-f-f-frank.

"Maya," she whispered, afraid speaking would somehow cause the snake to come closer. "What kinds of snakes do you have in North Carolina?"

"Wha—"

"What kind of—"

Then it didn't matter.

Because the snake grew. Its width expanded more and more while its tail shortened and that broad head enlarged. The thin, eight foot long serpent shifted, twisted and changed until it stood on two legs before her. Brown eyes. Brown hair. And two wide-spaced, thin, long fangs.

"*Help.*"

*

Wyatt tried not to growl at his Prime. The man had relevant questions that could only be answered by him, but Alex was keeping him from Bethy. He'd worked hard and saved to buy his home, and he wanted to be by her side as she discovered the different places that meant so much to him.

Instead, he was on the phone with Alex while he watched her through the window. Not long after she stepped outside, she'd pressed her cell phone to her ear, and he figured Maya was checking up on his mate.

Shit. She was his mate. Well, at least he was hers since she'd claimed him. He smiled at the memory. Twice. Regardless of the pain, she'd bitten him twice. Whether she realized it or not, the cat seemed to want to make sure *everyone* knew he belonged to her.

He couldn't wait to do the same to Bethy.

"Wyatt," Alex snapped. "Are you listening?"

"Of course, Prime." He was quick to respond. The last thing he wanted was for the Prime to come stomping over and interrupt his time with Bethy even further.

"Then answer."

He frowned and pinched the bridge of his nose, guessing at what the male wanted to know. "Bethy—"

"Who?"

He sighed. "*Millie* woke up this morning covered in dirt and bruises with a bite on the back of her shoulder. She doesn't remember how all that happened."

"What bit her? How can she not remember?"

"I don't know. To both. Some of her memory is returning, but it's slow going." Wyatt kept his attention on Bethy as he lowered himself into a chair. He could only see the top of her head, but at least he knew she was there. "She recalled my house and how she broke in last night," Alex grunted and Wyatt ignored the man. "But the rest is hazy to her."

"She's got problems, Wyatt. Are you sure—"

"She's fucking perfect." The snarl that burst to his lips startled him, but he wouldn't call it back for the world. "She's mine."

"Wyatt, I'm just saying—"

Wyatt's skin rippled, the lion ready to come out and play, to rip the words from Alex's lips. "Mine." He didn't recognize his own voice, but it didn't matter. "*Mine.*"

"Wyatt... Hold on a sec." The scratch and scuffling sounds coming over the line indicated that Alex covered the receiver with his hand. Then an echoing roar reached him as the Prime screamed a single word. "*No.*"

The male only used that tone when yelling at his mate. He wondered what Maya was up to now.

"Sorry." Alex cleared his throat. "I was saying that your mate has a lot of unfortunate history. It's something you should keep in mind when *things* happen."

"Are you insinuating she did this to herself? She somehow bit *herself?*"

"Wyatt, that's not what I'm saying. I'm saying she has abilities we don't understand, and her control is shaky at best."

The lion pushed and clawed at his control. It couldn't stand anyone doubting Bethy. It went against its nature to allow someone to badmouth her. "I don't know what happened to her, but—"

A panicked voice that sounded like Maya's reached him through the phone, and Alex's tone changed. His words were filled with anxiety. "Shit. Wyatt, where's Millie right now?"

Wyatt furrowed his brow. "Outside on the deck." He returned his attention to the back window, bitching at himself for letting his gaze stray. Except… Except she was standing on one of the chairs? What the…

Her body jerked and twitched then froze before tumbling from his view. "Shit. I gotta go."

"We're on our—"

Wyatt disconnected the call and dropped the phone, racing through the house as fast as he could. He hit the back door at a run, busting the panel off its hinges in a shower of glass and wood.

He skidded to a stop, bare feet slipping on the debris and sliding into his flesh. But the shards of pain were distant as he stared down at Bethy. Her face contorted, bits cracking and shifting into a perverted version of her cat. First one cheek, and then the other, her upper jaw snapping and changing before her lower jaw split and reshaped.

What was supposed to be a fluid transformation occurred in fits and starts. Her thigh bone went before her shin, her ribs before her spine was able to accommodate the change. Her legs shortened and thickened, forcing her to all fours before her paws could form.

And the pain… It seemed to pour into the air, filling it with her agony. It assaulted him with invisible fists, one strike on top of another.

106

Golden eyes framed in black focused on him. *"Help me."*

Human words from a half-cat mouth.

"Bethy." He sank to his knees, unsure where to touch her, how to soothe her, how to *help* her.

And still the shift continued. Patches of skin were slowly replaced by midnight fur, the paleness sinking into the dark. A change that should have taken a second took minutes to complete. When all was said and done, she lay on her side, panting and wrapped in her shredded clothing.

"Sweetheart." He edged closer to her, hand outstretched, when her menacing growl had him freezing. "Bethy, let me…"

The crunch of glass told him someone had arrived. He took a breath and tasted the air. Alex and Maya. Why the hell the Prime would bring Maya into this, he didn't know.

"Wyatt."

Bethy's growl intensified, and she rolled to her feet. It felt as if electricity filled the air. It crackled against his skin, flicking his arms and sliding around his neck before moving on. Apparently her power had weighed him and found him worthy. Alex's gasp told him Bethy's abilities found the Prime lacking.

Fuck.

He understood his mate better now, realized it wasn't specifically Alex that caused her reaction, but the fact that he was male. His sweet Bethy. So many men had hurt her.

"Bethy, stop." He glared at the panther standing feet from him.

The cat glared back and then turned its attention to Alex.

Fuck it. She was his mate. What she'd just experienced had been horrific, but they couldn't harm the Prime. He darted forward and

107

tackled the cat, forcing her to her back while he pinned her beneath him.

The cat snarled and snapped its teeth at him, the shining fangs missing his neck by a hairsbreadth. "Damn it. What's wrong with you?" He managed to snare one of her paws, but the other struck out at him, catching his sleeve and sliding down his arm. "What the hell?"

Wyatt sensed Alex approaching. Then another gasp came from the Prime followed by a heavy thud and then Maya's scream. He had Bethy pinned, but holding her physical body obviously didn't affect that *other* part of her.

Damn it, he didn't have time for them. Not when he stared into Bethy's golden gaze and instead found black eyes staring back at him.

Power, the part of her that came with being a Sensitive, turned on him while she bucked and jerked against his hold. She brought her back legs up, deadly claws spread and nails exposed, and aimed for his abdomen. He managed to corral her lower body with his left leg, pinning them to the ground, but it wouldn't last long.

She snapped at him again, this time her fangs catching his shirt, but thankfully, not skin. In frustration, she twisted and tugged, yanking one leg free of his grasp.

"Stop it." She got him again, and he grunted. Pain seared him, tearing through him like lightning, but he couldn't let her free. Not when she'd attacked Alex. He had no idea what she'd do to Maya.

"Calm the fuck down." He snarled at her, and she roared in return.

Blood trailed down his arms, flowing and dripping onto the wood beneath them, staining the surface a deep red.

Bethy's power scraped at him, attempting to tear into him, but it couldn't. For some reason, his body rejected her attempt to injure him. However, it didn't stop her from trying.

More of that prickling heat, more growls, snarls, and roars. She fought him with everything she had and still he held on. Minutes passed—or hours—and she remained his captive.

With no sign of peace in sight, he did the only thing he could do. And he hated himself for it. She'd spent years being forced to bend to another's whim. She'd spent day after day being beaten and abused so she'd do as they demanded.

He was about to do the same.

Wyatt allowed some of his change to roll through him. He willed his hands to claws and allowed fur to coat his arms, chest and neck. Next he urged the cat to transform his face, alter his human bones until the lion's snout replaced his mouth.

The moment he held the shape he desired, he lowered his head until it was less than an inch from Bethy's snarling maw. And then *he* roared.

Bethy immediately stilled, the black in her eyes fading into gold and fearful submission filled her feline features. A tremble shook her sleek body and then she relaxed beneath him, her paws no longer fighting for his flesh.

He wrapped one clawed hand around her neck and gently squeezed. Not to hurt, but to remind her a more worthy, stronger male held her captive. She immediately lowered her gaze and turned her head, attention shifting to the wooden floor.

With the assistance of his cat, he pushed human words past his fangs. "You need a powerful male and you've found him. I am your male. I am your mate. Everything inside you will become one and... You. Will. Submit."

Bethy whimpered, and another tremble slithered through her before piece by piece she became human once again.

As the shift reversed, a groan came from Alex, his Prime coughing as he regained consciousness. The first words from his leader's mouth hurt, but didn't surprise him.

"Clear the pride house. I want her in the cage."

CHAPTER *eight*

"The road to happiness is always under construction. But no worries, my SUV has four wheel drive. Let's rock this." — Maya O'Connell, Prima of the Ridgeville Pride and woman who is determined to have her happily ever after, damn it.

Millie woke slowly, climbing from the depth of her sleep and toward the light of day. Her body gradually came to life, shifting of its own volition as she struggled for consciousness. Unfamiliar aches and pains invaded her. The muscles in her arms throbbed and her neck hurt as if it'd been strained. A flicker of a memory shot across her mind... A flash of metal... dripping fangs?

A stabbing ache came from below her collar bone, and she brought her hand to the spot. Swollen. Two raised bumps just over two inches apart. Not big enough to be a mating bit from Wyatt, which meant...

Which meant something had bitten her again. She flipped through her memory, searching for who and how, but she came up blank. Nothing.

She shifted again, groaning with the effort, and then a warm hand pulled her fingers from her wound while the other hand brushed the hair from her face.

"Shh, Bethy. I've got you. You're safe."

When hadn't she been safe?

Millie forced her eyes open, demanded her body respond, and her lids parted. She blinked against the bright lights, but kept her focus on her mate. "Wyatt?"

"Hey, sweetheart." Worried filled his features. "How are you feeling?"

She furrowed her brow. "I hurt. My arms, legs." She brought her other hand to the wounds on her chest. "What happened?"

"You don't remember?"

"No, I," she furrowed her brow and thought back. "We were at your house. Alex called?" At his nod, she continued piecing together the snippets in her mind. "I went onto the back deck while you talked to him and... Maya called?" Another nod. "I don't-I don't remember much after that. I hurt." She did recall that. Pain, so much pain. "A lot."

"Nothing else?"

She shook her head. "No, should I?"

Wyatt's shoulders slumped, and he turned his attention from her which finally brought her focus on her location.

Bars. A long row of bars encased them, holding them captive in a large cage. The light glinted off the metal, each one catching her eye as her gaze shifted.

"Wyatt?" Panic threatened her, and she fought for calm while she prepared to fight back the cat and her power combined.

Except... they were gone. The dark cloud didn't lurk in its usual corner, and the cat was different. Present but muted and silent in its space, not reacting to their captivity.

Too bad the human part of Millie wasn't as calm.

"*Wyatt?*" She pushed his hands away and fought her coverings. Blankets were wrapped around her, holding her captive, and she battled the fabric.

With a thought, her claws formed, yet she didn't feel the overpowering surge of her cat wrenching control. No, it was as if the animal lent a hand changing a tire instead of stealing a car.

Ideas of slashing through her sheets vanished with the appearance of her claws. She stared at her paw, noting the dark fur that covered her hand, the midnight nails that replaced fingers and the soft pads that represented her palm. The fur stretched along her forearm and faded as it neared her elbow.

She brought up her other hand, comparing the human skin and fingers to the panther's paw. Then, with a whisper of a thought, she willed her pale hand to shift. And it did. Right there. Had she blinked, she would have missed the gentle roll as her beast did as she silently asked.

"Holy shit," she whispered.

"Yeah." Wyatt's tone held a hint of awe and pride.

"What happened?" At his frown, she begged. "Please."

He sighed. "I'll tell you, but let's get you cleaned up first."

"Cleaned up..." Millie turned her attention to her body, the claws forgotten. No, not forgotten. They were simply gone. A brief thought drifted through her mind at how much easier it'd be to remove her sheet with human hands. Then the fur disappeared, taking her claws with it.

She turned to her mate with wide eyes. "Whoa. What—"

"Clothes first and then we can talk about," he looked around the room, their cage, "everything else."

Realizing she wasn't going to get anything out of him, she nodded. That got him moving, rising from beside her and giving her a better view of the space.

She lay wrapped in sheets on a small, twin sized bed against the wall in their cage. The floor was concrete with drain grates every few feet. She craned her neck, wincing with the pain, and noticed a toilet, sink, and single showerhead hidden behind a curtain. A sparse cell.

Wyatt moved away from her and strode toward the bars, bending down and snatching something from the ground near the door. When he returned to her, she realized he held a bundle of clothing.

"Maya sent these along. She said the top might be a little snug since you're, and I quote, 'threatening her position as Queen of Booblandia.'"

Maya sent them? So the Prima knew they were in the cell. Had she put them here?

Instead of asking the questions lingering on her tongue, she nodded and accepted the bundle. She stood and shed the sheet, blushing as Wyatt's appreciative gaze traveled over her body. Rolling her eyes, she fought to ignore him and simply focused on getting dressed.

It was then she saw the damage. More bruises. Her legs and hips as well as a long, thick line across her chest that wove between her breasts. "What..."

"Just get dressed, Bethy." He murmured, and the other half of her nudged her into motion.

Not one third.

A half.

Stunned, she went through the motions, slipping on a pair of cotton, drawstring shorts followed by Maya's shirt that was, indeed, snug across her chest. By the time she'd wiggled the top into place, she was exhausted and slumped onto the bed in a flopping heap.

"Tell me."

"God, Bethy." Wyatt sat beside her and scooped her up, placing her across his lap. He took a deep breath and continued. "You were standing on a deck chair when I saw you through the window, but by the time I got outside, your shift…"

Another tremble and Millie changed position so she could pet and stroke his chest. "I'm fine, Wyatt. Whatever happened," she swallowed, sensing something horrible had occurred and hating that she didn't know what. "I'm fine."

"Do you ever remember your shifts? What they feel like?"

Millie shook her head. "No, the cat takes over and I'm sorta gone during the shift. Afterwards, I can see what's happening, but I can't do anything until she steps back."

"Good. Your shift was the most horrible thing I've ever seen. Your hands just now? That was normal. What you went through, Bethy, was something out of a horror movie." He took a deep breath and she nuzzled his chest, passing along any comfort she could. "And when it was done, your power attacked. First me, then Alex."

"Is he…"

"He's fine. But you and I fought. Sweetheart," something that sounded like a sob pushed through his chest. "I forced you to submit. I fought you. Those bruises on your body are from me. I wrestled you to the ground, pinned you, and demanded that you submit to me." He placed a finger under her chin, and she allowed him to direct her gaze. "I am so, so sorry."

Millie cupped one of his cheeks. "I don't remember it, but it was obvious I was out of control. Forcing me to submit to you was the right thing to do. We already knew my power doesn't really affect you, so you were the only one who could have done anything. And now," she shook her head. "Now it's all different."

"How?"

She removed her touch and held out her hand, willing fur to cover her skin while leaving the claws behind. "I can do this. The cat hasn't stolen control and is letting me draw on her without bulldozing me. And my power... It was so *angry* all the time. Furious with males and determined to keep them away. That's why it lashed out, and Maya figured out that forcing me to hold a child kept it restrained. It couldn't attack men while it was focused on protecting and caring for a kid. Now it's part of me, part of the cat." She shook her head. "It's not separate anymore. That big ball of rage is sorta... gone."

"That's good, love." He brushed a kiss across her temple.

"I'm assuming I'm in this cage because I attacked Alex. What's my sentence? Why are you here?"

He tightened his hold for a moment before answering. "Yes, you're here because you lost control, but you're not being sentenced. Alex wanted you contained while we figure out what caused you to—"

"Act like a crazed bitch." Millie glanced at the bruises not covered by her shorts. "Why haven't these healed?"

"That's another thing we're trying to figure out. We're waiting for Maddy to get here so that maybe she can take a peek inside and see if she can find something." Trepidation tinged every word.

"That's a good idea. I feel different. Changed. But my memory loss is scary." She brought her fingertips to her chest and brushed the wound. "Did you see what bit me?"

Wyatt shook his head. "No. Which is another thing we're hoping Maddy can shed light on. Maybe with her Sensitive abilities, she can take a look inside your head." He stared down at her, so much emotion filling his gaze that she rejoiced in the fact he seemed to mirror her emotions. "I was so worried, love. The shift, your power, your anger. It scared the hell out of me."

"I'm fine." His gaze strayed to her legs and paused for a moment on her bite, and she tacked on a qualifier. "Well, mostly."

*

A soft shuffle of a shoe scraping on the wood stairs had Wyatt tensing while a growl built in his throat. He quickly nudged Bethy onto the bed while he rolled to his feet and faced the basement stairs. He hadn't protested his mate being secured. She'd lashed out at Alex, and there was definitely something wrong with her. To his cat, understanding and accepting were two different things.

He let his weight settle on his toes while he kept his hands loose by his side. No need to be threatening while also protecting.

In seconds, the visitor hopped down the last two steps, and he allowed himself to relax a tiny bit. "Maddy."

"Hey, babes." The lioness winced and then turned back toward the stairs. "So help me God, I will neuter your striped ass if you don't quit it."

Ah, obviously her mate objected to her using a pet name and let her know it telepathically.

With a sigh, the woman turned back to him. "So," she rubbed her hands together in anticipation. "Let's see what we got. Millie?"

Wyatt reached back for his mate, and she readily took his hand, allowing him to lead her toward the bars. Her trust was such a beautiful thing.

When they reached the edge of her cage, his mate pulled her hand from his and reached through the bars. The simple move brought anxiety bursting through him. "Wait." Both women froze. "Will it hurt her?"

Maddy snorted. "If anyone gets hurt, it'd be me." That was followed by an eye roll before she turned to the stairs. Again. "No sex for a damned week!" She tilted her head to the side, obviously listening.

"Hah! Shows you! I've got a rabbit named Javier, and I'm not afraid to use him. He is my neon pink Latin lover, and I'm familiar with all of his tricks." Maddy stiffened. "You. Wouldn't. Dare." Even Wyatt sensed the woman's anger. "Come down here and say that to my face!" Then a grin split her lips. "Pussy!"

The woman finally turned back to them, and Wyatt fought his smile. His mate didn't have that problem. Her joy was like a physical thing as the emotions stroked his skin. With every moment she was happy, he sensed the feeling rise in him.

Maddy grabbed his mate's hands and then swayed. Her eyes rolled back in her head and a gasp escaped her mouth. That sound was quickly followed by the low grind of her teeth. She released Bethy and braced herself on the bars. "Whoa."

"What?" The joy vanished beneath his panic and the cat's fear.

The lioness shook her head. "Nothing. Let's try this again." She gathered Bethy's hands and swayed, but didn't nearly collapse this time around. "That's amazing."

"What?" Worry assaulted Wyatt.

"Shush, big kids are working," Maddy admonished him.

But he couldn't help his concern. Not when Bethy's eyes drifted closed, and she leaned toward the cage bars, as well. Her face paled and then flushed, the colors changing from white to deep red only to repeat the process once again.

"Maddy?"

Maddy ignored him and instead murmured to Bethy. "You can do it. Easy now."

A presence entered him, something ethereal inside his mind. It stroked his inner cat and ruffled his hair before sliding a hand along his cheek. He felt it, experienced it, yet he couldn't see the source. And then an overwhelming rush of emotion crashed into him. Hope.

Fear. Worry. Love. It encompassed him and yet he knew they weren't his.

Bethy.

"Good. A little too much there at the end, but you've got it." Maddy grinned. "Now let's see how others do." The woman slowly released his mate's hands. "This is going to be awesome."

Wyatt didn't like the sound of that.

"Ricker! Doll-face! Get that quarter-bouncing-worthy ass down here!"

Bethy snorted, and joy slammed into him. Another of her emotions.

The rapid thump of Ricker's booted feet on the steps reached them a bare moment before the tiger shifter emerged. The tiger's muscles were rigid and tense and the scent of his worry assaulted Wyatt. It was potent and furious, filling the room in a split second. The male was focused on Maddy, fear for his mate consuming him. It didn't matter that Bethy had never harmed a female; he'd obviously been worried.

Wyatt couldn't blame him.

However, the man's next action had him raising his eyebrows in surprise.

Ricker took a single step past the stairs and froze, eyes going wide and mouth hanging open before he staggered and fell to his knees. He slumped forward, hands colliding with the concrete.

"Holy shit." Then the man surprised the hell out of him. He giggled.

Maddy bounced around and giggled while clapping her hands. "Oh, better than awesome! You got owned." Maddy pointed at her mate.

Wyatt looked to Bethy, trying to figure out if her joy had somehow affected the massive tiger. Her gorgeous eyes settled on Wyatt, the

119

orbs changing from green to gold in a blink and then the scent of her need hit him. His mate wanted him, her sexual desire filling him with that single look.

A purr slid from her chest, and Wyatt felt his cat answering.

Ricker groaned and then gasped, the sounds followed by the aroma of the male's orgasm. That had his beast reacting in an entirely different way. Somehow his mate's emotions affected the male and gave him pleasure.

That could never happen.

Wyatt snarled and moved toward the door, fingers flexing while he called on the cat. It jumped forward, ready to destroy the bars and then the male who'd derived sexual release from their mate.

Maddy would probably be sad, but she could find another mate or a string of lovers. He didn't care. Ricker needed to be gone.

Maddy turned from her mate and focused on him with wide eyes. "Shit." The woman looked from him to Ricker and back again. "Shit shit. Millie-baby, tone him down or he's gonna get hurt, m'kay?"

"Huh?" His mate's voice stroked him.

"C'mon, switch the mojo around and tug on big, bad, and pissed the fuck off." The last word was followed by a nervous chuckle.

Good.

Then, just as his anger surged forth, ready to assist him in destroying the door, it retreated. It washed away into nothingness, sliding into the abyss as if it'd never existed. Contentment replaced the murderous emotion, and his cat settled into a low purr as its eyes drifted closed.

"What?"

Bethy's hand slipped into his, and she tugged on his fingers. "Chill out."

He looked down at her, at their joined hands, and then returned his attention to Ricker as he struggled to rise.

"What. The. Fucking. Fuck." The tiger growled as he pushed to his feet. A wet spot now stained his jeans.

Maddy helped him stand while bouncing in place. "Right? All kinds of awesome. Can you believe it? I mean, holy frijoles with guacamoles."

"Maddy?" The woman obviously understood more than any of them.

"Your mate right there?" Maddy pointed at Bethy. "Is the strongest, kicking ass-iest Sensitive *ever*," she propped a hand on her hip, "with control problems, and she's totally projecting. I mean, she's scary as hell, but I'd pay to see a repeat of that, like, all the time."

"But what about..." He let his words trail off.

What about the attack? What about the bites? What about the bruises?

Maddy's grin slipped, and her attention strayed to Bethy before returning to him. "It's hazy. I'm ninety percent sure the bite is from a snake. Maybe a shifter. Maybe not. But whatever it is, that's the cause of her memory loss." She shook her head. "I don't know about the rest. There's something there, but it's just out of reach to both of us."

Wyatt turned to his mate and sucked in a breath at the tears filling her eyes. "Sweetheart." He pulled her close and hugged her tight. "We'll figure it out. In the meantime, we'll get the guards looking for intruders in the territory."

"Wet," Maddy interrupted. "It smelled wet. Damp. Almost moldy. Like a towel that's been left in a wet heap too long."

Wyatt nodded his thanks. "Ricker, can you guys make sure everyone else knows?"

"Of course." The tiger's voice was deep and raspy, and he refused to acknowledge the hint of sexual satisfaction that filled the syllables.

"Good." He rubbed Bethy's back.

"Wyatt?" Maddy sounded hesitant, and he looked to her, raising his eyebrows in question. "Her cat needs a little boost to heal her. The snake's, guy's, whatever, bite kinda stunts that part of her. She healed quickly last time because she drank your blood."

He hated the heat that filled his cheeks. "You saw that?"

"Parts." She admitted and then sighed. "Okay, all of it, but at least your bits weren't exposed. I had to see Millie's tatas, and while they're gorgeous, they do nothing for me." She shrugged. "The point is, she needs a little chomper action to get her back to non-purple land."

Wyatt's cock thickened at the idea. Memories of their writhing bodies, the scent of her need and the feel of her coming on his hand filled his mind. Bethy rocked her hips, and he knew the same images flashed inside her head.

Nearby, Ricker groaned once again, and Maddy giggled as she clapped her hands. "I so gotta learn how to do that."

CHAPTER *nine*

"Practice does not make perfect. It makes babies." — Maya O'Connell, Prima of the Ridgeville Pride and woman who knows what the hell she's talking about when it comes to practicing and babies.

Need.

Need need need.

Millie was on fire for Wyatt, burning with desire and anxious to have his hands on her bare skin. His cock thickened and lengthened against her lower stomach, and her body heated in response. Distantly, she heard Ricker's groans and Maddy's giggles, but she only had eyes for her mate.

If Ricker and Maddy didn't leave soon, they'd get an eyeful.

Wait. No. No one should see her mate naked. They needed to leave. Now.

"Geesh!" Maddy yelled. "No need to get your wet panties in a bunch. I'm leaving, I'm leaving."

The sounds of Maddy's departure reached her, and she relaxed a bit. At least until the lioness's voice drifted back to her. "We're not going far, though. I so wanna ride your wave when you finally let go."

Millie smiled and nuzzled Wyatt's chest, sensing his confusion.

She spoke against his chest, a blush heating her cheeks. "They feel everything."

"Huh?"

"You feel some stuff. But everyone else feels it all as if my emotions were theirs. It will affect their bodies when we…" She shrugged.

"Maddy didn't seem too influenced."

"She's a Sensitive. She can block, or not, if she needs to."

"So, they're going to…"

Her face burned. "Ride the wave."

"And my blood?"

"Will help counter whatever toxins are in my blood." A sudden fear struck her, and she looked into his eyes. "I don't want you to let me bite you because it'd help me. I don't want to force you—"

"Sweetheart, taking your bite will be nothing but pleasure. I promise." He brushed his mouth across hers and then licked the seam of her lips. "I want nothing more than to feel your fangs sliding into my skin. I love the scars I have. I love that your cat felt the need to mark me twice. She's a territorial bitch, and I love it more than you could ever understand."

Oh, but she did understand. As a not-so-broken Sensitive, she sensed others' feelings. With the small effort moments ago, his emotions came to her. They couldn't speak telepathically like Maddy and Ricker, not until they fully mated, but sensing what was in his heart was easy.

The young boy who lived inside him was overjoyed that his mate wanted him, his mate claimed him so completely that he couldn't ever be tossed away.

Now that she had another heap of problems on her head, she wanted the same assurances. She no longer felt the need to destroy every male who came near her, but now everyone else experienced everything that passed through her mind. Before she was able to simply stay in Gina's little house and be perfectly content. But now, how far from people would they have to move in order to blunt her ability?

"None of it matters, Bethy." He lapped at her mouth. "Say the words and no matter what, I'll be with you. In town or two hundred miles from the nearest person, I'll be there."

The dam that'd been holding her back burst into a million pieces. Millie wrapped her arms around his neck and held him steady. She raised onto her tiptoes enough to bring their mouths close, and she whispered her demand against his lips. "Claim me."

Wyatt growled and fused them together. His tongue clashed with hers, tangling and torturing her with the burning kiss. He encircled her waist and lifted her feet from the ground, moving them across the room, and she trusted him to get them to the bed. Before long, her calves hit the bed frame and he lowered her feet to the ground.

Hands went into action now that they were no longer occupied by holding each other close.

Millie tore at his shirt, yanking the hem from his jeans and shoving it up his chest. Wyatt pulled at the waist of her shorts, tugging and pushing them past her hips. The moment they passed the roundness of her ass, they drifted to the ground. She stepped out of one leg and then kicked them aside, uncaring where they landed.

The moment his hands were done, she jerked at his T-shirt again, and he snared the fabric, lifting and tossing the top away in one smooth move.

And what was exposed had her breath catching in her throat.

Perfection. Utter perfection.

She ran her hands over his chest, tracing the lines of his pecs and then wandering on to the carved ridges of his abdomen. One, two, three, four... She kept counting, traveling south until the deep valleys of his stomach disappeared beneath the straining edge of the waist of his jeans.

And, oh God, his hips accentuated the juncture of his thighs, and she drooled at the idea of tracing them with her tongue, lapping at his skin until she got to his cock and...

Wyatt jerked, and the bulge in his jeans grew. "Damn, sweet, whatever that thought was, repeat it." He heaved in a breath. "But fully naked."

Millie shuddered at the heat in his gaze and rejoiced in the sexual power she held over this male. He was hers, but she didn't think she'd ever be worthy of a man like him. A man who was chiseled to perfection, who cared so much and demanded so little.

Again he caught her emotions and instead of urging her on, he growled low and grabbed her shoulders, shaking her gently.

"Never again." He bared a fang. "Whatever you're thinking, stop. You are mine. You are perfect. And you're mine." He wrapped an arm around her waist and yanked her flush against him. The thick ridge of his rock hard dick was unmistakable. A fully aroused shifter male held her close, and the desperate scent of his need filled her blood. "Mine."

His desire overwhelmed her, and she said the first thing that came to her mind. "You said mine three times."

"Because it's true."

Wyatt brought his free hand into her line of sight, showing her a single, sharpened claw. "Stand still."

She was prepared to ask why, but snapped her jaws shut with a squeak. He allowed her to ease back, and he placed the tip of the nail at the edge of her V-necked shirt. Without any effort, the claw sliced through the taut fabric, the top parting without a sound. With every centimeter traveled, more of her body was exposed until the T-shirt parted to reveal her abundant breasts and gently rounded stomach.

The urge to cover herself surged forth, but the need in Wyatt's gaze had her resisting her body's demands.

"You're gorgeous, Bethy." He brought his clawed hand up and tenderly cupped her breast.

The dark, black nails should have frightened her, but all they did was increase her arousal. He could easily slice her breast with his claw and yet she knew he would never injure her.

Her nipple pebbled with his ministrations, stiffening until the hard nubbin pressed against the center of his palm. "We need a bed, Bethy. Now. I need my mouth on these, sweets, and then I'm going to feast on the cream between your thighs."

He nudged her back, and she flopped to the mattress without hesitation.

"I did hear cats like cream." She grinned.

"Minx." He reached for the button of his jeans, and she licked her lips in anticipation. He wanted to taste her, well, she wanted to taste *him*.

"Cat." She smiled.

"My cat." He lowered the zipper.

His engorged cock sprung free, its thick, hard length jutting from his jeans. The plum shaped head was red and full of blood, a droplet of pale pre-cum decorating the tip. His heavily veined shaft seemed to beckon her tongue. She'd taste every inch of him, savor his musky flavors and then go back for more.

127

He left his pants clinging to his hips and nudged her into the position he desired. She lay perpendicular to the wall, her ass resting against the edge of the mattress while her head was by the wall. Her feet dangled and Wyatt used his body to force her legs wider.

"My cat. My cream." He dropped to his knees between her thighs. "And I want both."

"Wyatt…" She reached for him, and he pushed her hands to the blanket.

"No, love. I'm going to taste you and then I'm going to fuck this pussy." His amber eyes met hers, and he cupped her mound, pressing against her swollen, slick lips. "My pussy."

Millie whimpered and squirmed, shifting her hips and rubbing against him.

"You're so slick and wet, sweetheart." Wyatt rubbed her and she opened her legs wider. She wanted him, his fingers, his mouth, his cock. All of it.

"Please," she whispered and shuddered.

"Anything for you." He murmured and removed her hand, yanking a whimper of disappointment from her. "Easy. I just want to get my mouth on this pink cunt."

God—need raced through her—what his words did to her.

Wyatt stroked her inner-thighs, starting at her knees and running his hands along her legs. His calluses stroked and teased her warm skin, the rough touch adding to the need building inside her.

His thumbs teased the crease of skin where her thighs met her pussy, gently rubbing and tormenting her with the caress. With each pass, he eased closer to her damp sex lips. He tortured her, sliding up and then down, traveling to the very top of her pussy and then down to the curve of her ass.

Millie wiggled and squirmed, jerking her hips to the left and then the right in an effort to get him to delve deeper. All it managed to do was draw a chuckle from her mate.

Jerk.

Then he slid one thumb along the seam of her sex, softly tracing the line, and she trembled in excitement with the touch.

"Is that what you want?"

Millie shook her head. "More."

"Then look at me. Watch me taste you."

She hadn't even realized she'd closed her eyes or dropped bonelessly to the mattress. She forced herself onto her elbows and demanded her eyes open.

Oh, that was very, very wicked.

Pure amber eyes met hers, the hue telling her it wasn't just Wyatt the man making love to her, but also Wyatt the lion. Millie's cat perked up and purred, the addition of the beast gentle instead of overpowering.

"Good girl." He remained focused on her and then his thumb slipped between her lower lips, sliding over the slick inner-tissues and then...

She gasped and arched her back, sucking in a breath with the pleasure he created. He stroked her clit, pressing against the bundle of nerves.

"Yes," she hissed and then cut off the sound when he retreated. She whined and raised her head.

Wyatt grinned. "Eyes on me if you want to come, love. I'll make you scream, but you need to know it's *me* making you scream."

"It'd never be anyone else, Wyatt. Only you." Her mate gave an approving rumble and then his touch returned to where she needed him.

That thumb stroked her clit, rubbing the nub with gentle strokes. Back and forth, a slow glide that pleasured her without sending her flying to her peak. His caresses came in a steady rhythm, his attention on her. It was as if he tested her, ensuring she'd remain focused on him while she enjoyed his ministrations.

"More, mate."

Wyatt grinned and gave her what she craved. His touch transformed from gentle brushes to determined circles, sliding 'round and 'round her clit.

"That's it," her words came out as a hoarse whisper and she rolled her hips. "Right there."

"Here?" He circled her twice more and then suddenly fingers speared her pussy, delving deep into her heat. She jolted and screamed with the invasion, with the overwhelming pleasure it caused. "Or here?"

"Yes."

"Maybe both?" Now his fingers pumped in and out of her cunt while his thumb toyed with her clit. He fucked and stroked her, teasing and arousing her more and more.

And as he demanded, she kept her gaze on him. She continued to stare into his amber eyes, continued to watch the emotions on his face shift and change from one second to the next.

His gaze flicked to her pussy and then back to her. "Look at all that cream, love." He licked his lips. "I need a taste."

Wyatt's fingers disappeared, her heat now empty and her clit silently begging for him to return. And he did return. Except this time, it was so much better.

He pulled her thighs over his shoulders while he buried his face between her legs. His mouth first licked a path between her lower lips, tasting her from her pussy to clit and back again. He tormented her with his tongue, fucking her hole and then flicking her desperate clit. Over and again he repeated himself, licking, tasting, fucking.

With each movement, she cried out, begged and pleaded and demanded he bring her to peak.

Through it all, her eyes remained locked on his. Emotions battered her, his and her own, and she allowed herself to show him each one as it raced along her spine. That also meant she saw his. She sensed his increasing affection as it bordered on love. She accepted his worry about the changes occurring and knew he wanted to assure her happiness above all things.

Finally, he settled into a steady rhythm, his lips wrapped around her clit, providing gentle suction while he tapped the nub with his tongue. Two fingers slipped inside her, giving her a tender stretch while stroking her inner walls. He slid them in and out at a consistent pace. He fucked her with his hand, slowly bringing her to the edge of release. She panted and moaned, hands fisting the sheets, but she refused to lose her position.

"Wyatt... Please."

He growled against her pussy, sending her arousal spiking and her cunt tightened around his invasion. His eyes glowed brighter, and he repeated the sound, growling against her clit. Then that growl turned into a steady, rumbling purr and Millie thought she'd lose her mind in the pleasure.

Her body tingled from top to bottom, her muscles twitching and toes curling in anticipation of what was to come.

He curled his fingers, pressing and sliding them along her sheath in a gentle "come here" motion that caressed her G-spot.

"Yes!" She rocked her hips, meeting his shallow thrusts and riding his hand. "There. Soon."

So good, so fucking good. The sprinklings of pleasure surrounded her pussy, toying with her while it grew. Her cunt spasmed, milking his fingers, and she couldn't wait for them to be replaced by his cock. His purr intensified, the vibrations plucking her pleasure-filled nerves. Millie's cat responded in kind, the animal working with her as it voiced its affection for their mate.

Yes, this had to be what a normal shifter experienced.

Wyatt gave her a fierce, rough thrust, and she gasped. "Again."

He gave her what she demanded, increased his force and pace. Now he truly fucked her pussy, hand moving rapidly while his mouth kept up its maddening teasing. She took everything he had, took it and used it. Pleasure grew and grew while expanding to encompass her body. Already her muscles twitched and jerked in preparation of her release.

She rose higher, floating as the ecstasy increased and raced to her peak. With every breath, a new shudder of need attacked her and with every exhale she trembled. The edge was within sight, her pinnacle within reach. She stared down into her mate's eyes and read every emotion on his features.

He was a good male, a better man, and she had no doubt he'd be a devoted mate. Trusting in him, she allowed herself to be flung off a cliff.

"*Wyatt.*" Millie held her breath and the growling bubble holding her pleasure exploded, bursting and filling her with every ounce of pleasure she'd gathered. Her pussy milked his fingers in a rhythmic caress while all control over her muscles was snatched from her. She trembled and jerked, her toes curling as her orgasm stroked her.

She whimpered and whined, but his pace never faltered. He continued to torture her with his fingers and mouth, and she loved every moment of bliss he showered on her. It was beautiful, heavenly, and she realized she'd get to have this every day from this moment forward.

Slowly the delicious pleasure eased, Wyatt's tempo reducing until he was giving her gentle, occasional laps. When he slipped his fingers free, she sighed and slumped against the bed, a huge grin in place.

"Was that good, sweetheart?" he murmured against her mound.

"Yeah, but I know something better." She grinned.

His cocky chuckle filled the room. "What's that?"

Millie sat up, forcing him to ease back the tiniest bit. A glance down showed that his cock was as hard and delicious as she remembered. "I'll show you once the jeans are gone."

He raised a single brow in question, but rolled to his feet as she asked.

Perfect.

CHAPTER *ten*

"I'm never as bad as people think. I'm, like, loads worse. Times two." — Maya O'Connell, Prima of the Ridgeville Pride and a woman who finds joy in being very, very bad. You know, twice.

Wyatt looked forward to this, to the moment he could slide deep into his mate's mouth and fu—

Millie darted forward and engulfed his cock with her mouth, swallowing half of his length in one lightning-fast move.

"Holy shit!" He roared the words and forced himself to remain standing.

Holy shit was right. Her plump, pink lips were wrapped around his shaft and somehow the little vixen managed to smile while her mouth was filled with cock.

"Sweetheart." His voice was hoarse, his cat making speech nearly impossible. The animal loved that she would do this with him.

A lot of women didn't like tasting their male, and he'd never been so thankful to have found one that enjoyed it. Because, yes, she did. There was no mistaking the pleasure she derived from sucking his cock.

She slid along his shaft, his dick slowly emerging from her warm cavern only to be swallowed once again. She moved at a leisurely pace, the actions gentle, but no less pleasurable. Her tongue traced patterns on the underside of his dick, tapping and flicking his shaft with every journey forward and each retreat.

She varied her suction, pulling hard then barely suckling at all, varying her pattern from one moment to the next.

Wyatt fisted his hands at his sides, fighting to keep them from cupping her head and using her lush mouth. Except Bethy had other ideas. Ideas that involved taking his hands and gentling his grip. Then they were moved to her hair, and she forced him to fist the strands.

"Bethy, sweetheart." He shook his head.

She slowly eased back from his dick, exposing more and more of him until the head of his cock rested on her reddened lips. She lapped at the tip of his dick, and he shuddered, enjoying the pleasure of her tongue. His balls hardened and drew up against his body, pleasure forcing them to prepare for release. She flicked that sensitive spot beneath the head, and he trembled, fighting the need to come.

"Fuck, Bethy." She scraped a single fang along the sensitive head, and he nearly lost it then. "*Bethy.*"

"Wyatt?" He forced himself to calm and focus on her. "Fuck my mouth."

He immediately grabbed the base of his cock and squeezed, hoping to stave off his orgasm. "You can't say shit like that, love."

Bethy rubbed her tongue over his slit, and he squeezed his eyes shut, trying to imagine anything other than the sight of her licking up his pre-cum.

"But I want you to. I want you to fuck my mouth and then," she suckled the tip, and he groaned, "I want you to fuck and claim me."

"Shit."

136

He couldn't resist her then, couldn't have ignored her request if he'd tried. Doing his best to be careful, he gripped her hair and fed her his dick, watching it disappear between those plump lips. She moaned around him, drawing the same sound from his chest.

Bethy placed her hands on his hips and urged him into motion, showing him without words that she wanted him to dominate her in this way.

The cat was more than ready to meet her desires.

Slowly, unsteady and unsure, he flexed and slid deeper into her mouth. He watched more and more of his cock disappear and then reappear when he withdrew. His shaft glistened with her saliva.

"Damn," he whispered and repeated the move, a slow slide in and then out.

He watched for any sign of discomfort and found none. All he saw were eyes so full of trust and the beginnings of love.

He gradually increased his pace, making love to her mouth as pleasure rolled through his veins and gathered around his balls. She squeezed his hips, kneading them and urging him on.

"Sweetheart," he rasped the word and followed her lead.

It was ecstasy, bliss, and joy wrapped into one.

And then one of her hands disappeared. He watched her slide it along her body, between her breasts and over the mound of her stomach before disappearing from view.

Shit, his mate got off on sucking his cock.

"Are you rubbing that clit, Bethy?" His dick pulsed in her mouth, releasing more pre-cum, and she moaned around him.

Yes, she truly was enjoying herself.

"Are you going to come from sucking my dick?" Fuck it felt so good, so hot and right with her. "Rub that pussy, sweetheart." Her eyes remained focused on him, need and desire evident in her gaze. "Rub that cunt while I fuck this pretty mouth."

She shuddered, and he fought the urge to come. Not yet. He could enjoy her attentions, but he was going to fill *her* with his seed.

Wyatt tightened his hold and moved with her, catching the rhythm she used on her pussy and using it as his own. "Shit, yeah."

In and out, her mouth tightening and sucking him like candy as she pleasured herself. His balls throbbed, demanding to be released, but he wouldn't. Not yet.

He had so much more he wanted to do.

Pleasure increased, gathering steam the longer he used her mouth. He grunted and groaned, battling his body as it tried to embrace his orgasm while he fought to push it down.

A whimper surrounded him, and he recognized the look of her impending orgasm.

Growling, he forced himself to release her hair and pull her from his dick.

Damn, she was the most beautiful thing he'd ever seen with her eyes glazed with desire and her mouth swollen and wet from being wrapped around his dick.

Her hand still moved between her thighs and tiny whimpers escaped her lips. He reached down and snatched her fingers from their playground.

"The next time you come, it'll be around my cock, sweetheart." He grinned when she whined, but he wasn't going to relent.

A quick shove had his jeans falling from his hips. He let them puddle on the ground and then he kicked them aside. Thankfully, he'd shed his shoes the moment they'd entered the cage.

"Now, lay back and I'll give us both what we need."

With a whimper she scooted and turned until she lay back on the bed, head resting on the pillow and her legs spread wide. She showed him her perfectly pink pussy, the sex lips opening and exposing her delicious center.

His fangs lengthened and his cat urged him to take another taste.

But no, he had other things in mind.

Bethy was his and now he'd show her who she belonged to.

Nude, he settled between her spread thighs, resting on his knees. He reached down and stroked his dick, enjoying the slick slide of his callused palm along his shaft.

"I'm going to fuck you, Bethy."

She whimpered and nodded.

"And when you're coming around my dick, and I'm filling your pussy with my cum, I'm going to claim you." He let the bald words hang in the air. He knew she enjoyed his dirty talk, his plain way of telling her exactly how he wanted her.

Bethy shifted, legs twitching and thighs spreading even farther while she also tilted her head to the side, exposing her shoulder. "Please."

He could never deny her.

Wyatt grasped the base of his cock and pointed it toward her wet pussy. Leaning forward, he let the head of his dick caress her silken folds, sliding along her cleft. He slipped up and down, glancing her clit and then nudging her warm opening.

"Wyatt…" She whined and whimpered, and he thought those were the two most beautiful sounds in the world.

"Right here, sweetheart." He took a mental snapshot of his mate, the way her hair spread around her in a halo, of the passion filling her eyes and the red blush that consumed her cheeks. "Right here."

And with that, he gave them both what they desired.

Each other.

*

Wyatt lunged forward, and Millie gasped, the sudden feeling of fullness stealing her breath. His cock stretched and filled her needy pussy almost to the point of pain. But what a delicious pain it was. His cock slid deeper and deeper, consuming her from inside out, and still she wanted more. More of him. More of them.

She lifted her legs and wrapped them around his waist, settling her heels on his lower back, just above his ass. Tightening her thighs, she pulled him closer, urging him deeper until his hips rested fully against her.

The moment he consumed her, he fell forward, catching himself on his hands so he didn't drop his weight on her.

"Bethy," he released her name on a breathy moan.

She loved that about him, loved that he called her something different than everyone else. She was his Bethy. His.

"Take me, Wyatt. Make me yours." More than anything she wanted to belong to him.

With a growl, he eased his hips back and then shoved forward once again. He pushed deep and hard, sending her fat jiggling with the thrust. Part of her wanted to grab the pieces wiggling the most, but then his lustful gaze fixated on her breasts. He repeated the

140

movement, and his eyes seemed to glow with new desire as her tits bounced.

"Mine."

Millie slid her hands along his arms, enjoying the feel of his skin beneath her palms. So hot. So smooth. So strong.

He continued his slow yet rough pace. Gentle withdraw and powerful thrust, his focus never straying from her chest. Each one increasing the pleasure burning inside her. She scraped her nails along his arms, enjoying the hissing moan the move brought to his lips.

"Wyatt?"

He snarled, and she noted his fangs had begun their descent.

She reveled in the fact that she was able to drive such a powerful male mad with desire.

"Taste them." She brought her hands to her breasts and cupped the mounds, holding them in offering.

He didn't have to be asked twice. He moved quickly, gathering her nipple in his mouth and suckling her.

"Yes," she hissed. Right there. Just like that. He fucked her pussy and sucked her nipple in time with his thrusts. The two parts of her were connected, tied together as her ecstasy rose once again.

Unable to remain passive, she let her feet drop to the mattress, and she picked up his rhythm. She rolled her hips, meeting his thrusts with every tightening of muscle. Their bodies slapped together, the smack of skin against skin joining their breathy moans.

Millie released her breasts and scraped her panther's nails along his skin. She loved the red welts that trailed in her wake, loved the fact they seemed to drive her mate mad.

He snarled against her breast and moved faster. His cock stroked her dormant nerves, sending her rushing toward the edge of yet another release. She gasped with one fierce thrust and dug her nails into his shoulders with the next.

"Yes, yes, yes." She tossed her head side to side, lost in the pleasure of his body.

Her cat sent her a questioning purr, and she beckoned the animal forth, allowing it to join in their claiming. The cat wanted to bite and taste their male once again while also accepting the claiming bite from him. They would be tied together forever.

Millie rambled, alternating between begging and demanding while Wyatt feasted on her body and fucked her senseless. Her pussy spasmed around his invasion, rippling along his length, and each twitch shoved her higher.

It wouldn't take much more to send her over the edge, flying into a million pieces.

"Please, please, please."

He released her abused nipple with a soft pop. "What do you need?"

His voice was more animal than man, his cat taking more control just as hers did.

"Take me."

He pulled out and slammed home again, sending their metal bed frame trembling and grating across the floor. "Mine."

"Claim me."

He repeated the move, his ridged cock scraping her inner-walls. "Mine."

"Bite me."

He flashed his fangs and did it once more, the force shaking her entire body. "Mine."

Millie's body reacted to each one, burning hotter, soaring higher. The well of her ecstasy was nearly overflowing. "Prove it."

Two words meant to goad him and goad him they did. He went wild, and she went with him. Limbs tangled and fought while they demanded more from the other. They battled toward their release, their animals joining in with flashes of claws and fangs.

Sweat slick and breathless, she was balanced on the edge, so close and yet she needed a little more…

"Wyatt…" she begged.

And he gave.

Between one blink and the next, he struck, sinking his fangs deep and sure into her shoulder.

His bite was what she needed. She flew over the edge, pleasure overriding the pain of his claiming bite. Lava roared through her veins, burning with the immense joy of release. She sobbed and trembled, taking everything he gave her and aching to return the favor.

The scent of her blood hit the room, filling her nostrils, and her cat reacted, her fangs dropping fully. Without hesitation, she sank them into Wyatt's shoulder, giving him yet another scar to show others than he belonged to her.

Wyatt jerked against her, growling against her skin, and he thrust once, twice, and sealed his hips to hers. His cock twitched within her sheath and then she felt the warm heat of his cum against her inner-walls. He filled her over and again, each jerk forcing him to continue his release.

He trembled in her arms, and she hugged him close, gently rubbing his back as they recovered from their release and solidification of their mating.

A second ticked past and then another and then it was as if a rubber band snapped in her head. Suddenly she was filled with his thoughts, his feelings. Each one tumbled after another, tripping over themselves in an effort to move into order.

Above all, she found hope... and stirrings of love.

Wyatt shuddered and gently withdrew his teeth from her flesh, and she did the same, lapping at the new wound and encouraging the blood flow to cease. Once again she'd marked him and once again her cat was satisfied. It was also overjoyed at finally belonging to Wyatt.

He lifted his head, and she read those emotions in him, the hints of love now stronger than before while hope shone in his gaze. She cupped his jaw and urged him closer, uncaring of the blood coating their lips.

Shoving away her worries and self-doubt, she whispered against his lips, "Me too, Wyatt. Me too."

Millie pretended not to hear the echoing roar upstairs or Maddy's answering purr.

Because... eww.

CHAPTER *eleven*

"Alex is the pride's Prime so of course he's the boss. I gave him permission to say that and everything." — Maya O'Connell, Prima of the Ridgeville Pride and woman who likes to earn spankings.

The two of them spent the day making love. Come to think of it, they spent the night doing the same. Now Wyatt woke with his fully claimed mate in his arms.

A mate whose body no longer held even a hint of her injuries from the morning before. Sometime between their fifth and sixth round, he'd noted their absence. The biggest thing that thrilled the cat was the fact the mysterious bite had been wiped away.

His lion hadn't taken their mate being bitten by another very well.

But now she was wound free, and the only markings on her body were the claiming bites he'd given her.

Bethy was his and his alone.

He rubbed his hand along her spine, enjoyed the feel of her skin beneath his palm. She lay atop him; body draped over his and head resting beneath his chin. She was snuggled close as if she didn't want to give him a chance to escape.

She needed to realize there was nowhere he wanted to be but right there beside her. Well, except inside her.

Wyatt pressed a kiss to the top of her head. The cat was content, and he was filled with emotions that scared the hell out of him, but it was all good. Now they had to figure out where they'd live.

Yesterday revealed her power wasn't trying to attack every male, but it had done something else to Ricker. That "something else" pissed off his animal, but it wasn't like Bethy had done it on purpose.

His mate stirred, slithering her body against his.

Slithering…

Bethy moaned and stretched, then sighed as she relaxed against him once again. She snuffled his chest, blowing warm air across his skin, and the action had his cock filling. He'd never get enough of her.

"Mmmorning."

"Morning, love."

She hummed but didn't say anything else.

"How do you feel?"

She froze and remained quiet for a moment before answering. "Tired. A little sore." She sighed. "But my power," she shook her head, "it's all different. And…" she licked her lips. "Whatever you did to make it this way, I'm glad."

"But—" But he'd forced her to submit to him, to accept his dominance over her.

She shook her head, and he felt her determination continue to fill him. He wondered if it was this way for Maddy and Ricker. If they were able to share this intimate connection that allowed them to sense each other.

This and more. Bethy's voice filled his mind. *And I'm very glad you dominated the cat. I wouldn't be here with you if you hadn't. I'd still be hidden*

146

away, going crazy from dealing with my mind and body being torn in three different directions.

She shifted position and propped her chin on his chest. "I've never felt so at peace, Wyatt. Here with you, with my cat and power working together, I've never been so content and calm." He opened his mouth to reply, but she leaned up and nipped his chin. "Nope, no more apologies. Or then I'm going to have to start with how bad I feel about trying to rip out your throat."

His mate winked at him, and he relaxed into the mattress, accepting defeat. "Fine."

Bethy wiggled against him, rubbing her thigh along his and grinding her pussy into his leg. "Good, now that we've got that out of the way."

"Time out!" Maya's voice rang through the basement. "All kinds of I-don't-wanna-see-your-ass time out."

With a groan, his mate dropped her head to his chest. Her tiny hand partially shifted, small nails growing and darkening before she dug them into the mattress and shredded the sheet beneath them. A low, rumbling growl transferred from Bethy and into him, and the sound should have made him wary and worried about his mate losing control.

Instead, it made his dick hard.

Wyatt let scenarios roll through his mind. He wondered what he'd have to do to get the Prima back upstairs so he could have another hour or hundred alone with his mate.

"Don't make me come over there and bite your ass, Millie," the Prima threatened. "I didn't get my morning quickie, so you don't either."

The reason for his mate's anger bulldozed him, and Wyatt chuckled. "Prima, if you could turn around? We're not exactly dressed."

147

"You don't say. Millie's bare ass wasn't enough of a clue." His mate's growl didn't let up, and the Prima released an exasperated sigh. "Do you know how many penises I see in a day? I mean, Alex's is nice and thick and—"

"Maya!" Alex's voice rang down the stairs.

"Anyway, I see his and then there's East's and West's. Believe me, the last thing I wanna do is add to Penistown."

That drew a snort from Bethy, and Wyatt silently thanked the Prima. When he lifted his head to thank Maya for defusing the situation, he had to swallow his laugh.

She stood on the other side of the bars snuggled in footie pajamas with an ever-present carton of ice cream in hand. He raised a brow in question, and she rolled her eyes then shrugged.

"What? There's milk in here. And it's chocolate, so there's cocoa beans and stuff. It's like milk and veggies. Alex is making me bacon, so it's a totally balanced breakfast."

"Okay, then." Maya swallowed another bite and Wyatt asked the question that'd been niggling his mind since she'd appeared. "When did you guys get here? I thought you emptied the house and left after..."

After they locked him and Bethy in the cell.

The Prima shrugged. "After Maddy broke Ricker's penis—" A protesting roar came from above and Maya tilted her head back to yell. "After Maddy *bruised* Ricker's penis, but definitely did not ruin his manlihood-ness in any way," she lowered her head and returned her attention to Wyatt, "she called us and said we were all good. Bad Ass Millie McGee won't kill anyone with her magic mojo, but we may get the best orgasms in our life." She took another bite of ice cream and spoke around the spoonful of dessert, er, breakfast. "I call coming back to the house a win-win." She swallowed her bite. "And if you get randy after we all have a chit-chat... score!"

148

Bethy moved, wiggling and squirming and waking his cock up even more, until she too could see Maya. "Maya?"

"Yes?"

"Get the hell out," his mate growled. Any second now he'd come from her voice and growls alone.

"Well, that's not very hospitable. I let you into my home—"

"You locked us in a cage."

"Semantics. Plus, you were batshit and I don't have a padded cell." Maya tapped her chin with a spoon. "Though one would be good for the cu—"

"Maya!" Another roar from Alex and the Prima huffed.

"Fine, fine," she grumbled and stomped to the door. The rapid beep of the door's lock followed by a low thud told him they were no longer captive. "When you two are ready, we're all upstairs. Alex has some news and blah, blah. The door's unlocked and there's a set of clothes on the floor over here since someone shredded by favorite shirt. Cover the dangly bits and let's rock this."

Another bite of ice cream and she was gone, dancing up the steps.

When she finally disappeared, his Bethy focused on him. "She's like a fluffy tornado that sucks up all of the pink bunnies of the world and spits them out in BDSM gear."

Wyatt nodded. "Yes, yes she is."

Maya's raised voice could be heard through the floor. "Hear that Carly? You should be laced up in BDSM gear. Lemme get my crop."

* * *

Millie emerged into a new world.

149

Well, the same world, but every breath, every sight, was brand new to her. Now that she understood what Wyatt's cat had demanded of her, she recognized the changes in her mind.

She now had two pieces, but they were entwined, tied together so they were almost one with the other. The hate and anger she'd harbored were banked and shuffled aside. While not gone completely, the feelings were blunted, and she was able to easily recognize that each male she greeted didn't deserve her wrath.

It was freeing, beautiful, and all because of Wyatt.

Holding his hand as they crossed the kitchen, she allowed him to tug her along in his wake. She passed an annoyed Carly and a laughing Neal, then skirted a smiling Maddy with her scowling mate. Was he holding an ice pack to his crotch?

Maya burst into the room brandishing a crop as well as several straps of leather with silver chains dangling from their ends.

Millie *did not* want to know.

"I *knew* I had stuff from our aborted attempt at BDSM." Her eyes sparkled with mirth as she leaned forward and pretended to whisper. "Apparently, I'm not very submissive." She shrugged. "Who knew?"

"Everyone," the occupants of the kitchen responded, Alex included.

"What-ever." She plopped her stuff in the middle of the kitchen table. "So, Millie, you're no longer homicidal. Score one for the home team."

Millie opened her mouth to reply and then snapped it closed. What was she supposed to say?

"Um, thanks?" She raised her eyebrows in question as she looked to Wyatt.

Maddy snorted. "Don't thank her, she didn't do anything. That mate of yours did the heavy lifting."

Wyatt was plastered to Millie's back, his arms wrapped around her. His growl filled the kitchen, and everyone froze, Millie included, and the occupants slowly turned toward them.

"She. Is. Not. Heavy." He growled the four words.

Maddy gave Wyatt a deadpan look. "Seriously? That's what you got outta what I said? You need some protein or something." She flung a piece of bacon at him that Maya snatched from the air before it hit Wyatt. "What I *meant* was that you did the hard stuff. Geez, touchy much?"

Millie sensed the tension leave her mate, and she rubbed one of the arms wrapped around her waist, hoping to soothe him further.

"K. Now that we have our morning argument out of the way, everyone sit down." Alex nudged Maya, nibbling her neck as he leaned past her and placed a platter of food on the table.

Millie saw it then, saw the love they felt for each other and sensed how deep their bond went. Maya was overbearing, outspoken, and demanding, but Alex loved her for it.

The Prima caught her watching and Millie blushed, feeling like she'd intruded, but Maya shrugged. "It works with us. I say stupid things and he lets me hide behind him when I get in trouble."

Alex rested his now empty hands on her shoulders. "And I spank her ass and then thank God she's pissed off the right people. Because," he dropped a kiss to the top of her head, "by the time the Alpha or Buck, or whoever else and I are done commiserating about difficult mates, we've got a new alliance."

Millie leaned against Wyatt and pulled on the pool of her power, sending tendrils into her mate and found his thoughts and hers were in sync. They both wanted what the ruling pair had, and they were determined to work until they had it in their grasp.

She turned her head and twisted, dropping a kiss on his shoulder before stepping out of his arms. "Feed me, mate."

An amber glow overtook his eyes, and she knew she'd said the right thing. His animal was possessive and caring. It wanted to meet her needs, and the request immediately pushed aside any lingering anger over Maddy's words.

In moments they were all seated at the table, food being passed around while everyone talked over the other. She realized this was something else her life had been missing. When she looked to Wyatt, she sensed something similar coming from him. They'd both been missing this.

Under the table, she reached over and squeezed his thigh, smiling when he dropped a hand and covered hers. They had each other now and someday, they'd have their own family.

She couldn't wait.

The meal was filled with raucous laughter and good natured ribbing during which Ricker threatened to gut Maya. Alex asked to wait until she'd popped out another cub or two. He could have her after that if he wanted.

That had been followed by a whispered argument between the Prima and Prime with a not-so-quiet promise that Vaginaville was closed for the foreseeable—and definitely through the next fucking Gaian Moon—future.

It didn't take much time for the food to disappear into their stomachs, and then the conversation grew quieter.

"So, we're all gathered here today…" Maya kicked off more serious conversation.

Carly faux coughed, "Lame."

"Just so you know, best friend or not, I will so put rabbit back on the menu for the next run." Maya pointed at Carly and the rabbit shifter merely stuck out her tongue at the Prima.

"Enough." Alex cut through their needling. "Maddy has assured me that, beyond the fact you're transmitting rather loudly, you're no longer a threat to anyone. Between the incident yesterday at Wyatt's and your mating, you're now on an even keel."

Millie nodded. She felt that way. Well, she didn't recognize the transmitting part, but her anger and need to lash out at others was nearly nonexistent. "Okay."

"That means we're allowing you to return to Wyatt's with the understanding that Maddy and Elise will continue visiting you and work on your control. I know you were focused on that before, but I think that your mating to Wyatt has altered the plan a little."

Maddy nodded. "Yup, now you're more like a teen who's being overrun by hormones. Before you were… scary."

Millie blushed, but couldn't argue with the woman's assessment. It was true. "Okay. Did anyone figure out what…" She waved to her body. "What happened to me?"

Ricker sat forward with a wince, his one hand still beneath the table and she imagined him holding an ice pack to his crotch. "I went to Wyatt's and took a look around. Maya mentioned you asked about snakes?"

Millie nodded. "Yes. I remember one coming toward me and he… shifted?"

Things were still so fucking hazy, and it killed her.

"Sounds right." He nodded. "There were tracks near the window you used to break into Wyatt's home as well as around the back patio. We're lucky that it rained recently. The mud preserved them pretty well. We can't identify the breed, but it at least tells us you're not crazy."

Well, bonus points for that.

A memory prodded her and then it rushed forward. "After," she swallowed and cleared her throat. "The other morning, before I went to Wyatt's, I found a piece of shed skin in my room. At least, I think that's what it was. Will that help?"

Ricker nodded. "Yeah, it might. If we can narrow down species, it'll help us identify him. I found boot prints at the base of the stairs and tracked them through the woods. From what he left behind on the ground and on a few of the trees he passed, it's a male. He's just shy of six feet and about two hundred pounds. Brown hair, not sure about the rest of him."

Millie let the description trickle through her mind, and she felt the other parts of her react and flare to life. Her cat leaped forward to help them remember, but her power nudged the animal back.

No, no, no. She needed to remember.

Frank…

"Bethy?" Wyatt's murmur filled her ear.

"I… it's there, but they won't let it through. I see a face and then it's gone." Bland brown eyes, droopy eyelid, a scar across his face that the cat put there. The cat? Oh yes, her panther was rather proud of that injury.

Ricker nodded. "We'll keep an eye out."

"What… what did he do to me?" She had to know. "A snake bite couldn't have caused that reaction, right? I mean, Wyatt said my shift…"

"Was brutal." Maya's voice was subdued. "I've never seen anything so horrific in my life. I've helped free Freedom captives and seen

154

pictures of the things Alistair has done to others, but I don't think I've seen anything like that." The Prima shook her head. "I don't even know how you lived through it, let alone got jiggy with Wyatt later. I mean, I thought for sure you broke important girly bits with all that."

Millie rolled her eyes and then got serious. "Why was it that way though?"

Ricker dug into his pocket and winced, followed by a groan as he shifted his ice pack. Finally, he produced a small, glass vial. "This. I think his bite is what subdues you and forces the memory loss. The rest was probably what was in this bottle." He slapped it on the table. "I found this along with an empty syringe near where I lost his scent. He got into some kind of truck or SUV and left this behind. Whatever it is, I'm ninety percent sure it initiated your shift."

Millie rose and gently snared the bottle before returning to her seat. She rolled it between her fingers, seeing a few tiny droplets of the drug swirl back and forth. She brought it to her nose, intent on scenting it, when Ricker's words stopped her.

"You won't catch anything. We've all taken a whiff, and it smells like water. Like nothing."

Millie didn't doubt him, but she had to be sure. She eased it closer and inhaled, drawing what she could into her lungs.

The aromas slid into her, plucking her senses, and she found what she was looking for. Bitter. Sweet. Mold. Water. Rotting grass.

And then she was thrown into the past, thrown into yet another horrific dream.

Alistair walked into her cell, bringing a family member—a cousin?—with him. Then there was biting. Pain. Agony. Her body broken and destroyed.

"Goodbye, Millie-love. I'll be back tomorrow." Flat, brown eyes, droopy lid, evil grin.

Frank.

Without thought, she threw the vial, intent on getting it away from her as far and fast as she could. Thankfully Alex had fast reflexes as he plucked it from the air before it collided with the floor and shattered.

Millie clenched her shaking hands, and immediately Wyatt embraced her, pulling her close until she sat across his lap. He stroked her back, soothing her with his touch.

But her heart raced, worry and terror warred within her, battling for supremacy. Her cat roared, and her power pulled away, fighting to break her into thirds once again. It was Wyatt's touch that grounded her, but even that was weakening, the power he had over her lessening with every breath.

She would shatter again and again and again…

A sharp yank on her hair had her head wrenching back, and she was forced to stare into Wyatt's amber eyes. Fur covered his face, his features no longer that of a man, but of his lion. He snarled and bared his fangs, threatening her with his deadly teeth.

"Stop."

But the panic wouldn't wane, it wouldn't recede. He yanked again, baring her throat fully and forcing her to become vulnerable to him. But her panther and the dark cloud didn't care about his threats. He loved her, he wouldn't hurt her, not truly.

She felt her power rise, the cloud of anger gather and coalesce inside her. No, no, no…

A searing pain attacked her shoulder, the tearing of flesh sending agony blossoming through her body and the scent of blood stained her nostrils. The coppery fluid, her own blood, had the pieces of her stilling inside her. And then everything snapped back together as if they'd never been apart. She was one once again, and the mating bond between her and Wyatt glowed.

The golden thread entwined them, wrapping around their embracing bodies and tying them together even tighter than before.

He claimed her. He tied her. And she would submit.

Millie lay passive in his arms, letting him lick and lap at the new wound he'd caused, and it was then she noted the utter silence in the room. She turned her head to look at the others, but Wyatt's low growl had her freezing and she held her breath, waiting to see what he'd do.

The cat, now quiet and subdued, urged her to listen to their male. Well, she would, mostly. There would be times she'd tear into him, she was sure. But he was strong enough to handle all of her. So when she got out of control, when she neared the edge of sanity and her body threatened to tear into three, she'd always submit to him.

Wyatt ended his attentions with a gentle nuzzle and a soft sigh. He released her hair and rubbed her scalp while chuffing and purring. The sounds brought them out in Millie as well, and she nuzzled his chest, ignoring the new ache in her shoulder.

Silence continued to surround them. Well, at least until Maya spoke.

"So, now that you're back from kill-everyone land, care to tell us why you nearly went catshit?"

Millie furrowed her brow and turned toward the Prima. The Prima noticed she was also getting the same expression from everyone else.

Maya shrugged. "What, if she were a gorilla or something, I'd have said apeshit. She's a panther."

"You…" Millie wasn't sure what she was trying to say, but Maya waved her off.

157

"Yeah, yeah. I'm a different kind of Prima, this is a different kind of pride. I get it. I can't help that I'm awesome, and everyone else seems to have sticks up their asses." Maya turned to Alex. "Is that right? Sticks up their asses? I mean, stick up your ass is right, but sticks up their asses? It's plural and—"

Alex placed a finger over her lips. "Let's figure out what's going on and then we can discuss plural and possessive later."

"In bed?" The Prima's eyes brightened, and Alex nodded.

"In bed."

Maya turned to her and snapped her fingers. "Hop to it, missy. I've got a ride to catch, and it ain't in a car."

Smiling, Millie shook her head. These women, this pride, didn't seem to care how unstable she was. It appeared they were as fucked up as her, just in different ways.

Sobering, she voiced the name that had haunted her through her captivity. The cat and her Sensitive abilities could no longer keep it hidden from her. They were one, working together and no longer separately. The memories were hers once again and she called her past forward to the front of her mind.

All of the hatred for men she harbored wasn't caused by Alistair. Yes, he was the initial catalyst for her captivity, but he wasn't the male who'd broken her, destroyed her mind, and caused her to lash out at every other man she'd come across.

No, that honor went to one male. One shifter. One snake.

"It's Frank. Frank Mattson."

CHAPTER *twelve*

"The way to my heart is through ice cream. The way to Alex's heart… Well, it involves some kinda cream." — Maya O'Connell, Prima of the Ridgeville Pride and woman who is always ready to sate Alex's cravings. With food, people, with food. Okay, that's a lie.

Wyatt shook with rage. Even hours later, after they'd said their goodbyes and came back to his home, his body trembled with the need to destroy something.

Again the Mattson family, Alistair, had intruded on their town. Again, they tore and damaged their women. And again, they'd die.

Wyatt would be sure of it.

Two years ago, one of their own lions, Jenner Mattson, had participated in a woman's repeated rape and torture. At the time, he'd been working with his cousin, Alistair McCain. The woman in question eventually became a fellow guard's mate. Elise and Brute were happy now in Ridgeville with their pup, Katie, but it'd been a bumpy road.

Jenner was imprisoned by the council, but it seemed his father remained free.

Free to kill. Free to torture. Free to harm Bethy.

He felt a growl build in his chest while his lion paced and snarled in the back of his mind. They'd torture the male, fill him with those drugs and force the painful shift on him. Wyatt would smile and laugh while piece after piece changed and contorted, leaving the male in agony.

That would be... delicious.

Small hands gliding over his chest tugged him from his thoughts, but it was their travels to the waist of his pants that had him focusing on the present.

"Bethy?"

She rubbed her cheek on his back, spreading her scent on his shirt. "Hmm?"

Her fingers slid lower, wiggled beneath the hem of his shirt and then returned. Only this time her bare digits encountered his skin. They slipped over his lower stomach and dipped past the waistband. Wyatt sucked in a breath with the surge of arousal and the sudden filling of his cock. With that inhale came a wave of her need, the heated, musky scent of her cream invaded him and sank into his blood.

"What are you doing?"

The aroma of her juices increased. "Do you know how hot it was? When you bit me?" She purred against his back. "I was out of control, shattering, and you put me back together." Two fingers unsnapped his jeans. "So strong. So tough. So mine."

She lowered his zipper, the sound of the metal teeth parting joining her rumbling purrs.

"Bethy, we should..." She wiggled her hand into his pants and encircled his cock. *Oh, God.* "Right now isn't the time."

She squeezed him, pumping his dick. "Our job is to stay inside and stay safe." Her fangs scraped his back, and he realized that she'd sliced his shirt. "I want you safely inside me."

160

Shit, he almost came. Almost, but he held it back. "Sweetheart, you're not acting like yourself."

His mate had been a wildcat in bed, but he had to coax her there. She hadn't been aggressive and demanding until after a few orgasms.

"No, I wasn't acting like myself before, Wyatt. Now, I'm not afraid. I know you're strong enough to contain me. I know you won't ever let things get out of hand." She tightened her hand around him, and he released a low groan. "I know you love me enough to do what needs to be done, so I don't injure others. At least until I learn how to control the parts of me."

He grabbed her wrist and lifted her hand from within his pants so he could face her. He opened his mouth to tell her that yes, it was so fucking early, but he did love her. Or at least he was mostly in love with her. That eighty-three percent of him loved her?

Fuck it, she was his. Period.

Instead of saying all that, his mind blanked.

His Bethy was naked. Bare assed, all of those sweet curves exposed, and those pretty pink nipples hard and aching for his mouth.

"Bethy?" He squeaked out her name.

"Wyatt, there are parts of me that are out of control." She gave him a wicked grin, and he released a low growl.

His mate was naked, wet and ready for him, but she was also standing bare assed in front of the massive living room window.

Without hesitating, he bent down and placed his shoulder against her stomach before flipping her into a fireman's carry. At Bethy's indignant squeak, he smiled, and stomped through the house, intent on one destination: the master bedroom. Particularly, his bed.

He stormed past the kitchen and into the hallway, ignoring the spare bedrooms that were filled with random boxes. After ten years, he really needed to unpack.

Before long, he made it to his room, their room, and slowed as he neared the massive, unmade king-sized bed. Without hesitation, he flipped her off his shoulder and let her bounce on the soft mattress. Her fiery hair contrasted against the pale sheets while her curvaceous body called to him.

His cock, still hard as a rock, jutted from his jeans. He reached down and stroked himself, running his callused palm along his length. It kept his arousal at a simmering boil, just enough to tease, but not enough to push him over the edge.

No, he wouldn't reach his peak until he was balls deep inside his mate.

Smiling, his Bethy brought her knees up, exposing her pink pussy to his gaze. She ran a hand down her body, stroking between her breasts, over her stomach and then finally settling between her spread thighs. She teased her slit as he watched, fingers dancing along her pussy.

Damn, he wanted to be there, wanted to sink his cock into her heat and come deep inside her.

"What're you doing, Bethy?"

She grinned and slipped a finger between her sex lips. "Nothing."

That digit slid down and then back up, circling the hidden nub between her folds.

"Uh-huh." Shit, his balls ached and his cock throbbed. He tugged his dick and squeezed below the head. "Try again."

Bethy shook her head. Then that finger tap, tap, tapped her clit, and his sweet mate moaned, arching her back and rocking against her own hand. "Right there."

Somehow her thighs widened farther, laying her body out before him.

The tiny pucker of her ass caught his attention, and Wyatt knew what he wanted, what he craved.

Attention on her, he snared the drawer handle of his end table and tugged it open. A quick grab had his favorite bottle of lube in his hand.

At the sudden move, Bethy froze, her chest rising and falling in rapid succession. "What's that?"

Wyatt turned the bottle toward her. "Lube, sweetheart. Wanna know what I'm gonna do with it?"

She whimpered and shook her head. But he noted the hand between her legs didn't stop or slow. Nope, it sped up, tapping and circling her clit with an ever increasing rhythm. The fresh scent of her cream filled the air.

Yes, his Bethy knew. And she wanted it as much as he wanted to give it to her.

"How about I tell you anyway?" She whined in response.

He placed a knee on the bed and released his cock so he could easily move toward her. He kept making his way across the bed until he was between her legs, his bare cock inches from her wet heat.

And her hand was still going, still teasing her needy pussy.

"I'm first going to fuck you until you come on my cock." Desperate desire entered her gaze. Yes, she liked that idea. "And then, I'm going to turn you over. I'll nibble and bite your ass and *then* I'm going to stretch you so I can work my dick into your asshole." Bethy gasped. "Do you want that, sweetheart? Want my cock in your asshole?"

She whimpered and whined and finally nodded.

He tossed the lube beside her hip and then gripped her knees, pushing them wide. "Look at that pretty pussy." He salivated with the need to lap and lick her, drink down all of that cream. "Are you ready for me to fuck it, Bethy?"

She nodded.

"No, say the words."

Bethy licked her lips and whispered, "Fuck me."

He grinned. "Nice try. If you want it, you have to demand it. Be my strong mate, Bethy."

Power flared to life in her eyes, and he sensed her mounting desire. Her hand abandoned her clit and traveled farther south, digits sliding through her juices. She plunged two fingers into her pussy, pushing them deep.

"Fuck." She rolled her hips and shoved deeper. "Fuck me, Wyatt." She retreated and then plunged in once again. "Fuck my pussy and then… F-fuck my ass."

"Anything for you, sweetheart. Anything." Even if it meant he had to hold back his orgasm for hours. His dick was about to explode, the vision of Bethy finger fucking herself nearly sent him over the damned edge.

Without waiting for another invitation, Wyatt grasped her behind her knees and tugged her closer, resting the curve of her ass on his thighs. He placed the head of his dick against her opening, teasing her with a hint of penetration. Hell, he teased them both.

He inched in and then retreated, coating the tip of his cock with her juices. He'd never seen anything as beautiful as his shaft disappearing into her waiting cunt. She spread around him, stretched to accommodate his girth, and he wanted to live inside her forever.

"Wyatt." Bethy trembled and shifted, moving her hips in the process.

"Shh…" He withdrew his cock, shuddering as the room's cool air bathed his dick. He traced her slit, nudging her clit with the tip. "Is this what you want?"

"Please. Please please please."

Without pausing for a moment, he nudged his cock into her entrance and thrust forward, filling her in one smooth movement. Immediately she cried out, passion written across her features. Her molten heat surrounded him, blanketing him in the pleasure of her body. He took joy in the feelings she caused as well as in the pure pleasure in her gaze.

Balls deep inside her, he stilled, allowing her to grow used to his presence. Within moments she whined and squirmed. "Please, Wyatt…"

He slowly withdrew and then pushed in, relishing the tight squeeze of her cunt. Damn, he wanted to come, wanted to fill her with his seed.

But he had to save that for the last act. Her animal and power needed him to prove his dominance over her, and it'd be his pleasure to do so.

Wyatt gripped her thighs and held her tight, shoving back into her with greater force. She arched and screamed his name, her pussy rippling around him, milking him. God, it felt so good, he couldn't help but repeat the motion. Out and then roughly back in. He absorbed every whine and moan, every groaning plea.

He continued, hips slamming against hers, his balls smacking the curve of her ass. Sweat coated his brow and gathered on his chest. There was no way he was stopping or slowing. His mate would come for him. Period.

"Wyatt, Wyatt, Wyatt…" His name became her litany, the tone changed with each shift in position or strength of his thrust.

Fuck if she didn't come soon, it'd be over before it began, and they'd have to delay those darker things for later. But hell, he wanted in her ass, to take her that way and make her his.

Releasing his grip on one leg, he reached down and pressed his thumb against her clit. Her reaction was instantaneous. She screamed, bucking up and riding his cock with rapid rolls of her hips. She took what he gave and hell, he just went along for the ride.

It took two, three, and four brushes of her clit and she was crying out, body frozen in place as she came apart. She squeezed his dick so hard he couldn't decide if it was going to come off or simply blow because it felt so fucking good. His balls were hard and high, waiting for the word and then he'd come inside her.

Not yet, not yet, not yet.

Wyatt fucked her through her orgasm, drawing her feelings out as long as he could. Rough jerks slowly eased to random twitches and then she spasmed around him one last time before relaxing with a sigh.

Fuck, she was beautiful, all well-loved and wrung out from her release.

Now, he needed to give her another.

He ran his hands along her sides, rising higher to cup and knead her breasts. "Feel good, love?"

She whimpered and nodded.

Wyatt gently pinched her nipples and tugged on the nubs. "Want more? Want me in your ass?"

A whine in protest, but she nodded.

"Okay, love. Turn over." He eased from her welcoming wetness. His cock silently whimpered, but he'd been in her sweet, dark entrance soon enough.

Wyatt lifted her right leg and eased it around his front before helping her roll to her hands and knees.

Then, fuck, he was gifted the most beautiful sight in his entire life. Bethy's ass—white, pale, round and begging to be bitten. Fuck it. He repositioned himself behind her and before he even reached for the lube, he nibbled on one plump globe. Bethy squeaked in protest and then sighed when he licked away any sting he may have caused.

Damn, her skin tasted good. A hint of salty sweetness that had him salivating. He licked her again, taking in more of those flavors while teasing her with what was to come.

He made his way to the crack of her ass and tormented the sensitive flesh.

"Wyatt, don't." She jerked away, but he grabbed her hips and forced her to remain in position.

"Don't what?"

Her body heated and he imagined her face held a bright red blush. "Don't *lick* me *there*."

His sweet, innocent Bethy.

"Here?" He traced a path between the globes, delving deeper and lapping at the hidden skin. More of her scent surrounded him, invaded him.

"Wyatt…" she whined and now her ass was flushed red.

His poor mate sported a full-body blush now.

"Okay, sweetheart." He lapped at her skin once more before abandoning his playground. "Hand me the lube and I'll make you fly."

*

167

Millie immediately did as asked, snatching the discarded tube and holding it aloft behind her. She couldn't wait to feel him inside her. She was torn between embarrassment and delicious wickedness. He'd take her *there*, he'd be in *there*. Her satisfied pussy clenched on air, and she had to accept that her body was anxious for that possession.

The snap of the lube cap had her twitching, but she forced herself to remain in position, to remain exposed to her mate.

The cat was wary, circling and huffing as they lay prone for Wyatt. It was unsure, weighing their mate, deciding if he deserved what he was about to take.

Millie had no doubt in her mind. She definitely didn't have any when a cool, slick finger slid along her crack. She'd shied away from his mouth, still caught in the feeling of wrongness.

That digit circled her back hole, teasing the virgin flesh, and she tensed against his touch.

"Shh…" He stroked her back, soothing her, and she felt some of the tension leave her body. "Let me in, Bethy."

Bethy. His name for her. Because she was his. His. His. His.

The thoughts resonated with the cat, filling them both with the certainty they belonged to him and him alone.

She forced her muscles to ease, to relax beneath his touch.

He increased the pressure, and one finger slid past the outer ring of muscle, easing into her back hole. "That's it, sweetheart."

She trembled with the pleasure, the feeling of forbiddance adding to the growing bliss. He thrust in and out, a slow glide helped by the lube.

His other hand stroked her pussy, fingers finding her clit and thrumming the sensitized nub. "Oh, God."

He alternated his touch, rubbing the bundle of nerves while slowly fucking her asshole. She trembled and jerked, a shudder tearing through her at the illicit pleasure.

"That's it." His finger pushed deep and then withdrew, fully disappearing. She rocked back, whining with the loss of his touch. "Hush."

Two fingers stretched her hole now, spreading her, sending a slight burn through her body. But those digits on her clit... Fuck... They made it so much more than bearable. He teased and toyed with her, tormenting her with the opposing sensations.

Millie dropped her chest to the mattress, keeping her ass aloft while she sank into the bed. Let him do with her as he willed. She didn't care. It all felt so good, so right.

"Damn, that's beautiful." His voice was filled with true appreciation.

"Mmm..." she hummed.

His tormenting fingers disappeared again, but quickly returned as before. Yet this time, she felt three fighting for entrance, three pushing their way into her ass.

"Wyatt!"

"I've got you." He rubbed her clit with his thumb in tight circles.

"*Fuck.*"

The jerk chuckled. "Soon. Soon I'm going to fuck this ass and claim all of you."

The words resonated inside her, and the cat purred in response. Yes, that's what they wanted; they craved him branding her entire body with his claim.

The burn slowly subsided, her body adjusting to the three fingers and balancing along the edge of pleasure and pain. One nudge toward one or the other and she'd fall into that abyss.

"Please. I need you." Everywhere, anywhere, she *needed* him.

"You'll get me soon, sweetheart."

When he vanished this time, she tensed. His cock or another finger? She wavered between which answer she desired most. Then again, what did it matter? Either way, she had him.

Both hands disappeared, and she whined. No, no, no. She wanted it all.

The blunt, rounded head of his cock brushed her asshole, and the squirt of the lube bottle reached her. A squelching sound preceded the drop of cool fluid along the crack of her ass. Then his hands were moving, gathering it. She couldn't see, but she imagined him stroking his cock, coating it in lubricant before he pushed into her forbidden hole.

That had her pussy clenching and silently whining for attention.

Millie didn't hesitate to put her hand between her thighs, to revive the rhythm Wyatt had gifted her not long before. She circled and tapped, keeping her arousal at a delicious simmer.

Then… Then his cock pushed against her dark hole. It nudged and crept forward, forcing her to open and accept his penetration.

A sliver of fear struck her as a tendril of aching pain slid into her blood. "Wyatt?"

He was so big, so long, so thick…

"You can take me, Bethy. Relax and push out. I know you're being bad and touching that pretty pussy. Rub your clit for me." His voice was rough and strained.

Millie whimpered and focused on the feelings her fingers created. She noted the way her hips jerked when she scraped her nail over the nubbin and the way her cunt tightened when she tapped the bundle of nerves.

Wyatt thrust deeper, her hole spreading around his penetration, and her pussy clenched in response. It liked the hint of pain. It liked the wickedness. It liked having Wyatt inside her any way possible.

She did as he asked and forced herself to relax, to push out against his naughty invasion, and he plunged deeper inside her. Another burning pain attacked her, but the pleasure far, far, *far* outweighed any discomfort.

He withdrew a little, and she whined only to groan when he pressed back in once again. "Yes."

Wyatt gripped her ass, hands kneading her plump globes as he filled her farther. "Just a little more, Bethy. I'm so deep, sweetheart. Got my cock in your ass, and you love it, don't you?"

Millie whimpered and could answer with nothing but the truth: "Yes."

"That's good, sweetheart. Because I love being inside you like this." He withdrew and thrust forward, pressing in the last inch and then she felt his balls resting against her soaked pussy. Wyatt leaned over her, covered her with his massive body, blanketing her in his strength and scent. "I'm inside you now, Bethy. You're mine. All of you. Your mouth, your juicy pussy and this tight ass... You're *mine*."

"Yes." She was, wholeheartedly.

He scraped his fangs along the back of her neck, and she stretched, moving to expose more of her vulnerable flesh to his mouth. "All mine."

He lifted from her then, claw tipped nails digging into her hips as he held her steady.

Then it really began.

Wyatt eased half out before pushing deep once again, slowly fucking her forbidden entrance with long, sure strokes. His rhythm remained steady, and she toyed with her clit at the same maddening pace.

With every thrust, she tapped her clit and with every retreat, she circled it with the pad of her finger.

Tap tap, circle circle.

Again and again, his movements gently eased her arousal higher, giving gradual pleasure to her while keeping the ultimate prize out of reach. But she didn't care because it felt so fucking *good*. Like the damn Fourth of July was exploding around her clit and ass. His cock stroked nerve endings she'd never known she possessed.

But he kept her on that edge, in that place where her peak was *just* out of reach.

Millie rocked her hips, shifting her body in an effort to increase the power behind his strokes, the speed of his penetration.

The ass laughed.

"Nice try." He rubbed her ass. "Tell me what you want."

His voice was so deep, so full of sexual promise.

"Faster. Harder. Deeper."

Wyatt slowly withdrew and then slammed home, shaking both her and the bed. "Like that?"

"Yes. Please, yes." She wasn't above begging. Not when the cat was just as desperate as her.

He repeated the motion, pummeling her with his dick with three rapid strokes.

172

Slam slam slam.

Each one drew a sob from her chest, and she spread her thighs wider, offering more of herself to him.

"Please please please." She needed more and more of him.

"Like this?" He did it again, shaking their bodies with the power behind his thrusts. His balls slapped against her wet pussy, his cock pushing and stretching her spread asshole. She wanted it all, everything he had to give.

Instead of ceasing his torment, he adopted a new, rough rhythm. The slap and collision of their bodies filled the room. She panted and moaned, accepting everything he had to give to her.

"God, yes. Don't stop. Wyatt…"

The scent of his sweat and need filled the air, her own desire clouding his. His hands gripped her hips harder, the sting of his fingernails piercing her skin overriding the pleasure he caused.

Slam slam slam.

Over and over again, he dominated her body. "Fuck, that's it." He gave her three, rapid, forceful thrusts. "Like that."

"Yes. Don't stop. Need."

She needed so, so much.

Her orgasm was close, hovering within sight and a hair out of reach. She stretched for it, ready to embrace the euphoric feelings of her release.

"Come on, sweetheart. Come for me."

That was all she needed.

"Fuck!" She screamed the word as her world shattered. Her mind crumbled into a million pieces as pleasure stole her sanity. She trembled and spasmed, muscles jerking uncontrollably. Her pussy tightened in rolling waves, and her ass did the same. The ecstasy overrode everything, blinding her to anything beyond the pleasure pummeling her veins.

"God. Bethy. Love. Gonna." Wyatt jerked against her in short, rapid thrusts and finally sealed his hips to hers with a bone rattling roar.

His cock swelled inside her, stretching her the tiniest bit farther, and it was enough to toss her back over the edge once again. Another orgasm tore her in two, filling her with the bliss of release. She shuddered and cried out, overwhelmed by the sensations he caused inside her.

"Wyatt!" She sobbed his name and then he was there, leaning over her, hand snaked beneath her and across her chest while his teeth...

Wyatt claimed her once again, fangs embed in her flesh, tying them together even tighter than before.

A single, garbled word reached her. "Mine."

Yes, yes she was.

CHAPTER *thirteen*

"It doesn't matter if I win, I just wanna make sure the other guy loses. Killing him ensures that outcome." — Maya O'Connell, Prima of the Ridgeville Pride. She swears she was never this bloodthirsty. It's the twins. Bringing those little parasites into the world made her evil.

Wyatt wasn't sure what woke him, what had his cat snarling and shoving at him to get the hell out of bed. They'd made love for hours, fucked hard a time or two, and finally passed out in a messy heap.

Somewhere along the line, he'd decided loving Bethy was the smartest decision he'd ever made.

Now he was awake, muscles tense and fur lurking below the surface of his skin. His gums ached, the animal ready to lend a hand.

But why?

He remained motionless, allowing his beast's senses to assist him where his human sense of smell and hearing wasn't up to par.

Nothing seemed out of order or odd. The wind rustled the trees, and he heard the occasional call of a bird. The soft scuffle of a paw on grass reached him, but he recognized his fellow guard's gait. Brute lurked nearby. The man had a personal vendetta against the Mattson family and had been happy to lend his assistance. The lion hoped for a chance at Frank Mattson.

Wyatt wasn't going to tell Bethy when the guards came on duty and when they'd moved their positions closer to the house. She'd get all embarrassed at their chance of hearing them and then she'd get mad. He liked his balls right where they were.

Still, something pulled him from sleep.

He opened his eyes, letting the light of the moon guide him as he looked around the room. Everything looked the same, nothing out of place, yet his cat was ready to tear meat from bone.

His heart rate picked up, muscle banging against his ribs as adrenaline rushed into his bloodstream. Sweat leaked from his pores, and impotent anger filled him.

The cat sensed an intruder the man didn't. An intruder the guards hadn't yet discovered.

Then he heard it—the telltale shift of fabric along the scaled skin and the hiss that only came from a snake. The cloth near his foot shifted, and Wyatt waited. Bethy's body was entwined with his, front practically fused to his side, and the last thing he wanted was to risk her.

Seconds ticked past, and he forced his body to remain neutral, demanded his breathing remain even and steady as the snake, Frank Mattson, approached.

Soon, he told himself.

Closer, closer, closer. The slim body slid along the bed, slowly growing heavier with each flex of muscle. Fuck, the asshole was shifting, changing so that when he finally hovered above them, he'd be human once again.

Shit.

Bethy sighed and rolled from him, her pale body bared to the room and the snake paused. Frank's low hiss filled the area, and the slight weight seemed to double. Shit, Wyatt realized he didn't have any more time to waste.

With a massive push, he kicked the intruder to the left and shoved Bethy to the right. His mate rolled over the other side of the bed and landed with a pained moan. He only had a split-second to worry about her before the real fight intruded on him.

A half-shifted Frank collided with the dresser, cracking the furniture and sending knickknacks flying. The male now stood tall, built exactly as Ricker described. His human skin was covered in deep green scales while his nose was flattened and his head wider than normal. Frank opened his mouth wide, flicking out his tongue and exposing his long, thin fangs. Saliva dripped from their tips, and Wyatt wondered exactly how much was spit and how much was poison.

He really didn't want to know.

The snake hissed at him as he pushed away from the dresser, and Wyatt's cat responded. His body grew, muscles bulging and thickening while fur sprouted from his pores. His hands transformed into a lion's paws with deadly claws spread. His mouth became the beast's snout, animal fangs crowding his human teeth.

Partial transformation complete, *he* hissed.

Unfortunately, Frank seemed too crazed to be afraid. Dumb ass snake. His lion was about to take the male down and then they'd burn his remains, destroy him and get rid of him as if he'd never existed.

Frank was the first to move, snake darting across the seven feet that separated them as if it were nothing. One moment he rested sprawled against the dresser and the next he was striking out at Wyatt. The snake's clawed fingers barely missed his shoulder, but a miss was a miss, and it gave him a chance to retaliate.

He punched the male, fist driving into Frank's stomach with one heave. He followed it with a quick crack to his jaw that had the man's head whipping to the side. Wyatt took advantage and went after him again, this time using his claws and scraping them along the man's chest, digging deep furrows into his flesh.

Frank released an anguished cry and retaliated, hands flying and nails flashing in the room's dim light. A movement to his right snared his attention, and he saw Bethy standing on the opposite side of the room. She clutched the sheet to her body, and pure terror coated her features.

Oh yes, Frank would die for scaring his mate. Soon.

A hiss brought him back to his fight, and he caught the strike aimed at his neck, wrapping his fingers around the male's wrist. Frank's nails seemed to glitter, the snake's scales adding to the affect. Holding tight, Wyatt took the opportunity to wrap his furred paw around the man's throat.

Distantly he heard the heavy thumping of a body slamming against his front door. He imagined Brute trying to get into the house after hearing the crash of Frank colliding with the dresser. For the first time in his life, he cursed himself for being so damned worried about security. Brute would never break through. There was no way he could come into the home via the windows, the fucker was too big. Plus, they were impact resistant and meant to hold off a damned hunk of wood going a hundred forty miles an hour. The back door had been replaced by material equally strong.

Damn it. He'd have to handle Frank by himself, and then he'd soothe Bethy.

Tightening his hold, he choked the slippery snake, cutting off his air. The green scales darkened under the pressure, and his lion gleefully roared at Frank's impending death.

Except... The snake suddenly jerked, kicking Wyatt in the stomach. He released Frank in surprise, and that's when the man struck. The sharp, reptilian fangs dug into his forearm, sinking deep and he felt the moment the poison entered his system. It burned its way into his veins, scorching every nerve ending as his heart pumped it through his body.

He slowly felt his grip on his body lessening, the muscles no longer responding to his mind's orders. When Frank released him, Wyatt dropped to his knees. Pain overwhelmed him, the burn of Frank's poison searing him from inside out. His blood boiled and his heart pumped the venom deeper into his muscles. It tore at him, seeping into the hardness of his bones. It attacked his mind, hunting and searching for his memories, but his cat fought the liquid death.

The animal refused to lose consciousness, refused to allow someone as pathetic as Frank force them to forget his Bethy.

His lungs froze as the full weight of the situation struck him. He hadn't protected her, hadn't kept her safe as he'd promised. Pain not related to Frank's poison invaded him, overrode the agony of the venom.

His heart. His heart broke and cracked under the weight of what was to come.

He believed in his mate's strength, had faith in her ability to fight and survive.

Yet that attitude didn't brush aside the fact that she now had to face her greatest nightmare come to life… alone.

She'd suffer for his arrogance, his belief that nothing could invade his home, nothing could get past him and harm his mate.

Wyatt fell to the side, body frozen by the poison yet his mind cataloged everything that happened within his line of sight. It was strong enough to disable him, but there was nothing that could erase his memories of Bethy.

He saw Frank's cocky smile.

Saw that grin turn evil.

And then he saw something he'd remember the rest of his life.

His Bethy, sweet and timid when she wasn't raging at males or screaming for more, held a wooden bat in her hands. And she didn't appear to be afraid to use it. Bethy raised it high, hands holding the grip so tight her knuckles were white, and then she screamed.

*

"No!"

Millie felt as if her world were crumbling right before her very eyes. Oh God, Frank had somehow snuck into the house. They hadn't found him and he'd snuck in— No, slithered. The asshole snake crept into their home and he'd bitten Wyatt and...

No panicking! I can't help Wyatt if I panic.

Thankfully, she'd tripped over a baseball bat and shoes as she'd rolled from the bed, and now she was ready to bludgeon the man to death. And fuck it, she didn't even feel guilty.

Millie brought it down, swinging in a short arc aimed directly for the snake's head. She'd hit him over and over and over until he couldn't ever hurt her again. She felt the cat rising within her, her power right behind the beast, and she prayed for calm. She couldn't lose control, not when Wyatt needed her. Let her remove the threat and then she could shatter into a million pieces.

But damnit, Frank spun and grabbed the barrel of the bat, stopping her before it struck him.

"You stupid bitch." He yanked and jerked it from her hands. "Did you think you could actually hurt me?" Frank shook his head. "No, baby, you're mine. My mate, remember? Mates can't hurt each other." He smiled wide, exposing his bloodstained fangs.

Frank took a step forward, and she eased back. "No," she shook her head, panic threatening to overwhelm her. But she had to do this. For herself. For Wyatt. For them. "I have a mate. Wyatt is my mate."

The snake hissed. "You're mine!" His reptilian tongue flicked out. "I've claimed you over and over, baby. Your cat is having a hard time accepting me. But I figured it out. I fixed the formula and now she'll want me." His eyes were glazed, crazed. "I'm sorry the others hurt you, but I have it right now. We'll be so happy together."

Hands now empty of a weapon, worry assaulted her. He had his natural poison on his side. A glance at Wyatt showed it'd already worked its way through her mate. She couldn't protect her male if she was bitten, as well.

Millie's fingers tingled and burned, and her panther snarled in the back of her mind. Wait, she did have a weapon of her own. Her power stirred, midnight black and rolled with fury. More than one weapon.

Weapons she'd never actively controlled. Fuck, what a trial by fire.

"I'll never be yours. Never!" She shook her head, punctuating the statement. "You forced yourself on me, Frank, but you're never going to do it again."

"Honey…" He stepped forward and she moved back.

"No!" She allowed her hands to change, let the cat flow through her and shift her hands to lethal claws. The beast then moved on to her face, changing her human visage to a bastardized version of the panther's head. Midnight fur replaced her pale skin, and she knew she faded into the shadows with the change.

Panthers were sneaky bastards, and she embraced that side of her.

Her beast fed her the cat's agility and hunting instincts.

"I'm not your 'baby' or your mate. I'm nothing to you." A snippet of her past overlaid the present. Frank's nude body, the sweat that

181

coated him, the flex of muscles as he sought release… "And you will never touch me *again*."

Frank's gaze drifted to her hands and she was satisfied to see the surprise overcome Frank's features along with a hint of fear.

"Baby," he soothed. "What are you doing?"

She knew what she was doing. Killing him. "Did you hear me? Never again."

Her power responded, satisfied and urging her to finish him, to destroy the male who'd harmed them over and over through the years. He drugged her, tortured her, and her human mind had been unable to handle the pain.

He was the reason she was always angry. He was the reason she struck at every male, friend or foe. He was the reason she was so fucking broken.

That enraged her. That he'd done things so horrible her mind splintered and broke from his treatments.

Millie called on the black cloud within her, beckoned the very core of her Sensitive powers, and allowed it free reign. That part of her surged and spanned the distance between her and Frank, diving into him like a starving beast. He jerked as if physically struck, body listing to the side as he stumbled.

"What-what are you doing?"

More images, snapshots of his past actions came to her.

Her blood decorating the floor. Her wrists bleeding as she fought her bindings. His fangs sinking into her body over and over again in an effort to mate her.

Millie pushed them all back. She and the cat had other things to do. Like gut Frank.

"Do you remember how I spent my eighteenth birthday, Frank?" She cracked her neck and flexed her hands, stretching her claws and settling into the newly shaped bone and muscle. She was strength personified in this shape, her curves not detracting from her deadly intent. "Beneath you." She raised her hand and extended her paw, smiling as the light glinted off of every nail.

"You can't—" He winced and coughed, grabbing his head. "You can't do that. What are you doing?"

"Do you know how you'll spend tonight?" Frank didn't answer her question, but she wasn't surprised. "Beneath *me*."

Millie sprang forward, tackling him to the ground in one leap. He'd hurt her, violated her, and injured her mate.

Clawed paws dug into his muscles, sinking deep before tearing at his flesh. She ignored the rotten stench of his snake's blood and instead focused on injuring him, killing him. One gouging scratch became two, became four. His claws scraped her body, and she recognized her injuries, but pushed them aside.

Hurt. Kill. Two words, repeating over and over.

Frank jerked and heaved, rolling her beneath him, and he straddled her waist.

The panther didn't care, not when she had her Sensitive powers on her side. That part of her was fully fused in her mind, reacting to her every thought as she dug through the snake's mind. Horror after horror flicked past, and she ignored them as best she could, but they wouldn't be silenced.

Her fourteenth birthday.

Frank backhanding her.

She turned fifteen.

Frank tying her down.

She never had a sweet sixteen.

Not with Frank braced above her as his venom went to work, his body straining as he fought to keep her still so he could…

Oh, God, eighteen…

Frank keeping her captive as others entered her room.

Millie struggled to shove the memories aside. They wouldn't help her defeat the male.

Frank hissed and bared his fangs, leaning down as if to strike and wound her as he'd done to Wyatt.

Wyatt…

She spared a split-second glance at her mate and noted his wide, panicked eyes. Well, yeah, she wasn't enjoying this shit either. Her wounds burned and she was ready for Frank to die already.

"Millie, you're not being a very good girl."

Very good girl?

Three words, another memory. Frank's blood tinged hands stroking her bare stomach, tracing the lines of her ribs and then finally cupping her cheek. She was naked, beaten, bruises decorating her body. *"You're my very good girl."*

She tore herself from the past and back to the present. Her cat and her power had endured enough. The two assisted her, the dark cloud of rage lashing out at Frank while her cat reacted with inhuman speed. She twisted her wrists in a sudden move and then shoved his chest, sending him flying backward. She didn't spare time for a breath before she launched herself at him, pouncing like the panther inside her.

Again and again, her ball of rage pummeled him, disabling him, and she took her chance. Opening her jaws wide, she attacked. Teeth sank through flesh and bone, goring his throat in a massive, powerful bite. She increased the pressure, grinding down on his spine until fangs met her lower teeth.

She wrenched then, tearing out half of his neck with that fierce pull. Dark blood pumped and sprayed from his body, soaking into the wood.

But it wasn't enough. Never enough. The cat wanted to bite again, wrap its maw around his skull and pull until it jerked free of the snake's body.

Even now his tainted blood coated her mouth, it seemed glued to her tongue and clung to her throat. Millie gagged on the spoiled taste, but its presence signified eventual death.

Yet the cat wasn't satisfied. Her animal wanted to gorge on his blackened blood, ensure Frank could never return. It ached and pined for his lifeblood, and she fought the cat's instincts.

The rapid pounding of feet on the carpet reached her, and she shifted her stance, preparing for a new attack. She straddled Frank, crouching low to let the newcomer know the snake was *hers*.

A man jerked to a stop inside the doorway. She breathed past the rancid blood and scented him. Lion. Familiar lion.

Did he want her prey?

Her power followed her line of thinking and lashed out at him, sending him to his knees. Prey was hers. She'd earned the right to destroy him with every wound he'd inflicted and every moment of pain she'd endured.

The stranger groaned and gripped the doorknob.

A moan behind her snared her attention, and she curled her lips back, ready to defend herself. Only... it was her male. Her male injured, yet stirring. His gaze met hers, and she noted his control returning, his limbs moving determinedly.

"Bethy, stop."

Stop what? She wasn't doing anything.

The lion near the door pushed to his feet. No, he wanted her snake. So she struck again, sending him to the floor.

"Damn it, Bethy. Don't make me do it." A growl filled her mate's voice. Good, he was recovering well. But what would he do?

Millie nudged the snake's head, sending it lolling to the right. Frank's pain-filled eyes met hers. It was then she noticed his hands clutching his throat, his blood continuing to flow past his fingers. Maybe she'd watch him suffer as he'd gleefully watched her year after year.

She sneezed, clearing the stench of his blood from her nose and then refocused. Her prey clung to life, but it'd be over soon. She looked down at the body beneath her. Scaly. Thin. Probably tough.

But hers.

She licked her muzzle and grimaced at the rotten taste. She didn't want it though. Movement to her right caught her attention, and she swung her head around. She glared at her mate. She was happy he was rising to his feet, but he couldn't have hers. She'd killed it, damn it. Well, almost. But even if she didn't want it, no one else could have it.

She bared a fang, curling her lip and flashing it at Wyatt in warning.

He froze in place. "Bethy, you need to relax, sweetheart. Step away from Frank. He deserves to be sent to the council for what he's done. Let them interrogate him. Let them sentence him."

Her. Prey. Besides, he'd be dead soon. She'd bitten deep and took quite a bit of flesh with her.

She flexed a paw and then rested it on Frank's chest. She dug her nails into his flesh one by one until all four were sunk deep into him.

She dragged it down, exposing more of the man's muscles and blood.

Wyatt's next words were tinged with his lion's growl. "I'm begging you, sweetheart. Calm down now."

She'd earned the right to destroy him. Earned it through blood, sweat, and tears. So, so many tears.

The longer he lay beneath her, the more of her memories returned.

There wouldn't be anything left of him to burn.

The stupid lion by the door stirred again, and Millie released a wailing roar, sending it vibrating through everything in the room.

A heavy weight collided with her, slamming into her side and sending her rolling and scrambling away from Frank's body. She fought to get her feet beneath her, blood-slick paws sliding on the wood floors, her claws fighting for purchase. That same weight settled atop her, holding her down when she would have risen.

She growled low, let the threatening sound pulse through her, but her assailant didn't move. No, it returned the sound, attempting to scare her into submission.

Millie shifted and jerked her legs, digging her nails into hardened wood and fighting the body atop her. It didn't budge, but did growl once again, the attacker's moist heated breath bathing the back of her neck.

The move had her stilling, freezing in place. He'd tackled her, caged her, and stood poised to end her life in a single bite. A shudder tore through her, a hint of fear finding its way into her body.

It wasn't the lion by the door; he was still in sight.

No, it was... she inhaled, drawing in the scents of the male above her. Her mate. Her mate held her captive.

Traitor.

He was keeping her from her prey. Her. Prey. She snarled, releasing a furious roar that bounced off the walls of the room. At the same time, she pushed up with her legs, bucking and trying to get him off her body. But he retaliated, struck her and dug his teeth into her flesh. Not deep, not truly painful, but just enough for the scent of her blood to fill the air and a stabbing ache to pierce her mind.

Millie tensed, her mate's jaws around her neck and teeth threatening to end her life. She didn't move, didn't make a sound, as she fought to figure out his intentions. The cat wanted to fight, wanted to continue the battle, and yet…

Wyatt growled around her vulnerable flesh, and it sank into her bones, crept along her spine and filled her from paw to tail. When she remained, he repeated the sound, deeper and longer, and tightened his jaws. Another shard of pain tainted her blood, and she fought against the instinct to submit.

Hers. Hers. Hers.

He shifted his stance, weighing her down with more of his body, and then the lion's groin rested atop hers. They were in the right position. Her male could mount her, take her, and claim her in this form.

That thought, that consideration, was what tore Millie's human half from the back of their shared mind and straight to the fore. She forced the cat to acquiesce to Wyatt's dominance, to tilt their head to the side and go limp beneath him.

She was *not* into furry sex.

The moment she let her body go lax, his bite eased, and his large, feline tongue stroked her neck and lapped at her wounds.

Slowly, her human thinking emerged in full and took over for the cat. She nudged her body into shifting back. She urged it to release

188

the animal and return to the form their mate would appreciate most. Her body slipped from one form to the other, fur slithering into her skin, and bones reforming to her human visage. In less than a second, her furred shape was replaced by her nude, human body.

Wyatt shuddered above her, releasing her neck, and then his skin was plastered to her back. He caged her, surrounded her with his massive body in a show of both dominance, and love.

He was their male. He was their mate. But above all, he was theirs.

CHAPTER *fourteen*

"Everyone is entitled to their opinion, but if it doesn't agree with my opinion, you might not make it through the night. Now, what were you saying?" — Maya O'Connell, Prima of the Ridgeville Pride and official keeper of the opinions. Be careful, if you disagree with her, she will cut you.

Millie refused to leave the bedroom. Re. Fused.

Nope, nothing doing, wasn't happening, she'd be content to live out her days locked in Wyatt's spare bedroom. She glanced around the area, some of her belongings littered the space now. They'd transferred some of her stuff while she'd showered Frank's tainted blood from her body.

Wyatt stayed with her, alternating between calming her and ordering her cat to keep itself in line. She'd been unsettled, broken and shattered by the events. She hadn't been witness to the cleanup, but she'd heard the comments. The whispered words of the males who tromped through the house had easily reached her.

Savage.

Crazed.

Dangerous.

But she wasn't, not really. Now… now she was more centered than she'd ever been. The cat was still frayed around the edges. Her power still spiked and jerked here and there, but the urge to kill and maim had fled after she'd realized Frank was well and truly gone. Not dead, but incarcerated forever. Somehow he'd survived and been life flighted to a trauma hospital that specialized in shifters. He'd never speak again. She prayed they'd take her suggestion and remove his fangs. Permanently.

Now she waited to find out if they'd remain in Ridgeville.

She'd attacked Alex.

She'd gone after Brute.

She'd nearly ripped the head off a male.

She only felt bad about two out of three, if she was honest.

Wyatt didn't harbor an anxiety that matched hers, but he said he'd go wherever they needed to go. Whether that was in Ridgeville or elsewhere.

She was his home.

The thud of a fist striking the front door told her Alex had arrived. She wondered if he'd bring Grayson, his Second, with him. It seemed like an event the male needed to be involved in. He'd been traveling a lot, splitting his time between Ridgeville and Chicago while also hitting other shifter groups. He'd been off "forming alliances" for the pride.

Based on gossip, he'd been hiding and keeping his distance from Honor. Gossip *also* said the two of them were mates. Millie figured time would tell. Or not, if she wasn't allowed to stay.

Dangerous shifters risked being put down or exiled. It might be kinder to Wyatt to have her life ended. At least he'd still have his pride to lean on.

The front door thumped closed, and she paced, nibbling her thumb as she strode from one side of the room to the other.

Deep voices came to her, Wyatt's low baritone easily distinguishable. It'd only been two days, and she was already tuned to him. The door muffled their words, keeping her in suspense, but she'd know soon enough.

The creak of a floorboard sounded from outside the room, and Millie froze. Adrenaline flooded her veins, fear rising hot and fast inside her.

Had Frank come back?

She should have killed him when she'd had the chance. It would have taken one more bite, one more tug and his head would have—

The doorknob turned, and she didn't give a damn about her irrational fears. They were fears. Period.

The wooden panel eased open, the hinges squeaking as it slowly swung away from the jamb. Her fingers tingled, the cat sneaking forward. It'd hidden after the previous night's performance, knowing it'd taken things a teensy bit too far. The throat biting thing had probably been enough. Nearly gutting him after the bite was what worried others the most.

Yeah, she had a small rage issue.

Finally a face peeked around the edge, and Millie found herself looking at familiar blond hair, familiar blue eyes, and a very familiar, very mischievous smile.

"Maya?" She opened her eyes wide.

The Prima placed a finger over her lips and ducked back into the hallway, only to quickly reappear. "I only got, like, a second."

She crept all the way in and waved her hand in the hallway. Then more women appeared, one pride mate after another slipped into the room.

"They're gonna figure out I'm gone soon. And then they'll realize we brought the cavalry." Her grin turned into a broad smile. "I've been waiting to call in the cavalry for*ever*."

"Prima, you don't understand." Hell, *she* didn't even understand.

Maddy bounced forward. "I understand. You totally ripped that guy's head off. Well, almost. I don't even have the words to explain the level of awesome you achieved."

"Totally," Carly agreed.

"Honestly, if that'd been an option, I would have done that to Alistair." Elly, Deuce's mate, shrugged. "I only got to shoot the man. Brains do make a nice mess, though."

As one, the women froze and Millie held her breath. Shit, shit, shit. Tess, mate to Harding and Alistair's semi-daughter, was in the room. From all reports, she hated the man and suffered a lot of abuse before he'd been killed, but still... *her father.*

"Eh, I would have paid for pictures," she quipped and the tension was swept away.

All right then.

Millie waved to the only other woman in the room: Elise. Brute's mate. His mate. And they were in the same room. "Elise, I'm—"

"Nope, no apologies." Elise nudged her way toward Millie. "None at all. He's fine. Sore and cranky that a woman kicked his ass with her mind, but that's pride talking. Nothing was broken, and all of his downtown bits are in full working order." The fox waggled her eyebrows.

"You're sure?" Doubt still lingered.

"Absolutely. Quite sure. Six times, in fact."

Okay then.

"We're getting off track here. We have a schedule." Everyone fell silent at Maya's shushing. "And by schedule, I mean we need to hurry our asses up before we get caught."

That sent a round of snickers through the room.

The Prima hopped toward the bed and flopped onto the mattress, then patted the soft surface. "C'mere. We brought presents."

"Maya, I don't—"

Maya rolled her eyes. "Sit already."

Millie gulped and did as ordered, slowly stepping to the bed and easing down where the Prima indicated.

The lioness swung a massive bag onto Millie's lap, and she instinctively caught it. "Hold that for a sec. It's got presents. We all contributed something." She dug into the bag and tugged something from its depths. "Aha!" She held the small object high. "Now, I get that you're kinda bitey, so I snared a few of these at the pet store before Alex got up this morning."

Maya dangled the object in front of Millie's face, and she raised her eyebrows. "Um, thanks?"

"Oh, it's awesome. See?" Maya wiggled it around. "It's flat, so when you shake it, it's like dead prey. And you can gnaw on it. That means you get the dead thingy feeling along with sating the bitey needs. Win-win." She dove into the bag again. "I actually used them with the twins to teach them how to hunt and kill and it was great. I mean, I didn't wanna get bloody all the freakin' time, right? I also taught them how to play 'fetch', but don't tell Ale—"

"Maya." The masculine voice was soft and level, no hint of emotion in the single word, but everyone focused on the source, on the massive, powerful male that stood in the doorway.

Millie gulped and wiggled away from the Prima.

The Prime was too controlled and she sure as hell didn't want to be around when he lost it.

"Yes, love?" The Prima grinned and batted her eyelashes. "Are you pissed about the kitten toys or playing fetch? 'Cause I gotta tell ya, I think we've got the most bloodthirsty kids in the pride. Keep that in mind while you yell at me. I think you should be thanking me for helping them develop their—"

"Maya." Oh, that time he sounded really, really pissed. "I'm more concerned about my mate sitting beside a homicidal panther." Alex looked to her. "No offense."

Millie shrugged. "It's true."

Maya snorted. "Puh-leeze. She didn't kill the guy. Almost, but not quite. Anyway. *Big furry deal.* I almost ate Andrew in the freakin' meat department at the grocery store when I was changed. And then I would have happily gutted that whore-ific tigress."

"But you didn't," Alex countered.

"Elise shot a guy in the head. Oh!" Maya raised her hand. "And Harding's dad in the knee." The Prima looked so smug. "Then, remember when Millie's brother Ben got all beaten to hell and killed because Tess kept secrets. That's almost homicidal in a weird, twisted backwards way." Maya nodded and turned to Millie. "My bad about bringing up your dead brother, by the way, but I'm trying to save your ass."

"Um, okay?" Millie wasn't sure what she was supposed to say to that one. While she felt bad for Ben's actions, he'd been her brother by blood, but she didn't feel any guilt. They hadn't grown up together; she'd barely remembered him. And yet, he'd remembered it all. The gift and curse of elephant shifters.

"Anyway," the Prima waved her hands around. "Alex," she rose from the bed and waltzed up to her mate, seeming not to care about his anger.

Well, Millie cared. A lot.

"The point is," Maya poked her mate in the chest, "you men mated a bunch of whacked out, crazy, homicidal, seriously awesome women. So, if y'all think you're gonna waltz in here and be all 'Me Tarzan, you Jane' on us, you're delusional."

"Maya?"

"Oh! Let's not forget Carly! She's a freaking rabbit shifter, and she *stabbed* Alistair and wanted to hunt up a voodoo priestess to see if we could resurrect Andrew so she could kill him again."

"Maya?" The Prime crossed his arms over his chest.

"If you don't think *that's* fucked up, I don't know what to tell you."

"Maya?" He spoke once again, and Millie saw a hint of a smile lurking around his lips.

The Prima huffed. "What?"

"Millie's staying."

Millie's heart froze, the muscle no longer pumping blood through her body. Her lungs stopped drawing air into her body. Her world ceased for a moment as the Prime's words rattled around in her brain.

Millie's staying.

Millie's staying.

Millie's staying.

"As you said, if we kicked every crazy, homicidal woman out of our pride, there'd be no one left."

The Prima opened her mouth, and Millie wanted to scream at her to shut it. She didn't want Maya threatening Alex's decision. "Bite me, Lion-o."

In one swift move, Maya was lifted and tossed over Alex's shoulder. The other women scooted out of the way, and the Prime carried his mate into the hallway and, she assumed, out of the house.

The last thing they heard from the Prima was: "You ass-sniffing, butt-crack licking, litter box-using fuckhole!"

*

The final strains of Maya's yell echoed through the home and Wyatt still stood frozen in the kitchen.

They were staying. Millie had to promise to work with Maddy and Elise on her control, but she'd been planning on that anyway. She was also "encouraged" to remain close to Wyatt until she'd gone through a few weeks of training with the two women.

They were newly mated, so he didn't feel like keeping his mate close was a hardship. He hoped to keep her *naked* and close.

A fist pounding against his front door got him into motion, and he strode toward the front of his home. By the time he got there, the damned thing was bowing and cracking beneath the strain.

Wyatt opened it and ducked when Ricker's fist came dangerously close to his skull.

The tiger opened his mouth and snarled at him. "Where the hell is she?"

He assumed the male was looking for his mate. A glance behind Ricker revealed that the rest of Maya's guards had shown up on his doorstep.

Wyatt stepped back and pointed to the other side of the living room. "Down the hall, first door on your right."

Male after male tromped past him. Ricker was in the lead, followed by Neal, Brute, Harding, Deuce and… Grayson?

He raised his eyebrows at the pride Second as he strolled into his home. "Honor's not here."

The man shrugged. "I know. I wanted to keep these guys under control. Alex called and asked Ricker if he knew where his mate was. We happened to be training and a worried shifter…"

"Is a deadly one." Wyatt nodded. "She's not dangerous."

Well, much.

Grayson rolled his eyes. "I know. No more dangerous than any of the others, anyway."

Wyatt took a moment to really look at the pride's Second. He'd aged in the two years since realizing Honor belonged to him. He'd spent more time away from the pride than with it, and it was wearing on him. New lines of worry dug themselves a home around his eyes and between his eyebrows.

God, he couldn't even imagine the pain Grayson had endured all this time.

"You okay, man?" The men in the pride weren't all touchy feely, but damn the guy looked rough.

Grayson quirked his lips and shrugged. "Better than some, worse than others."

"Is there anything—"

Feminine squeaks and outraged yells preceded a round of masculine chuckles and the distinctive sound of a hand hitting someone's ass. Ricker strode into the room first with Maddy tossed over his shoulder. The others immediately followed, Carly over Neal's, Elise over Brute's, Tess over Harding's and Deuce held Elly in the cradle of his arms.

199

"Hey! Why does Elly get to be all snuggled?" Maddy cut through everyone's objections, and they became united in their annoyance.

"Yeah, how come Elly…"

"She's two breaths from giving birth, that's why." Elly stuck out her tongue and blew a raspberry. "So, pft on you."

A round of grumbled "lucky bitch" and "traitor" rippled through the women, but then they returned their attention to bitching at their own men.

Before long, they'd all filed past Wyatt once again, leaving him with a weary Grayson. "I mean it, man, is there anything I can do?"

"Help her grow up a little faster?" Grayson gave him a sad smile. "Man, I'm fine. It's hard being here with her. I'm heading back to Chicago in a couple of days. Distance makes it easier."

With those few words, Grayson left the house. Wyatt stood in the doorway, watching the men wrangle the women into their cars and trucks. Before long, they were pulling out of the driveway and leaving Wyatt to his peace. With Bethy.

The soft shuffle of her bare feet on the wood floor announced her presence, but it was her scent that had the cat stretching and waking. A small hand slid over his back, followed by her arm and then she was leaning into his side. Her scent welcomed him, lured him in and begged him to stay.

He wrapped an arm around her shoulders and tugged her even closer before dropping a kiss to the top of her head. "You okay?"

Bethy nuzzled him. "I'm getting there. You?"

"Sweetheart, having you with me is so much more than okay."

She tilted her head back, and he stared into her eyes. "Alex said I get to stay."

"I know."

"The women said I'm no more batshit crazy than them."

True, but he wasn't about to say it out loud. He liked his balls and those women *were* batshit crazy. "Yeah?"

Bethy nodded.

"Okay, then. Alex wants you to stick close for a while."

"Until I'm a little less batshit and only regular crazy?" She grinned, and Wyatt answered her smile with one of his own.

"Yeah."

The rumble of a motorcycle starting up cut into the morning's silence, and they looked back toward the driveway. To the man straddling a Harley looking alone as Wyatt had once felt.

Now Wyatt's life was filled with love and passion and hopefully, someday, a family. All the things Grayson didn't have and wouldn't have until Honor hit her first heat. For the male's sake, he prayed it'd be soon.

"Is *he* going to be okay?" Bethy's soft voice drifted through the motorcycle's rumbling.

"Maybe."

He felt her power rise, their mating allowing him to sense her feelings, and he detected her sliding into the pride's Second. Grayson's muscles relaxed a fraction, some of the tension lining his body easing and settling into a more natural position on the bike.

As quickly as it'd darted away, it came back to her, and he heard Bethy's sigh. "He will be."

His Bethy. Selfless. Protective. Dangerous as hell and that made his dick rock fucking hard. But also so damned caring it made his heart

201

hurt. He'd never deserve her, never be worthy of her, but he sure as hell wasn't letting her go. Ever.

Even with a foster family growing up, he'd been so fucking alone.

And now he wasn't.

"Hey." Wyatt grabbed a lock of her hair and lightly tugged until she looked at him. "Love you."

Tears filled her eyes while her emotions bowled him over. The same feelings of unworthiness, happiness, and joy filled her and spilled onto him. "Love you, too."

Fuck it. They had a family: each other.

The End

If you enjoyed Big Furry Deal, please be totally awesomesauce and leave a review so others might discover it as well. Long review or short, your opinion will help other readers make future purchasing decisions. So, go forth and rate my level-o-awesome!

If you enjoyed this book, here are some links to help you hunt up the rest of the Ridgeville series:

Ridgeville #1 – He Ain't Lion (FREE) http://bookbit.ly/halzon

Ridgeville #1.5 – You're Lion http://bookbit.ly/ylzon

Ridgeville #2 – Ball of Furry http://bookbit.ly/bofzon

Ridgeville Series Volume One – Ridgeville 1, 1.5 & 2
http://bookbit.ly/rdg1zon

Ridgeville #3 – Head Over Tail http://bookbit.ly/hotzon

Ridgeville #4 – Fierce in Fur http://bookbit.ly/fifzon

Ridgeville #5 – Deuces Wild http://bookbit.ly/dwzon

Ridgeville #6 – Sealed with a Purr http://bookbit.ly/swapzon

Ridgeville #7 – Like a Fox http://bookbit.ly/lafzon

ABOUT CELIA KYLE

Ex-dance teacher, former accountant and erstwhile collectible doll salesperson, New York Times and USA Today bestselling author Celia Kyle now writes paranormal romances for readers who:

1) Like super hunky heroes (they generally get furry)

2) Dig beautiful women (who have a few more curves than the average lady)

3) Love laughing in (and out of) bed.

It goes without saying that there's always a happily-ever-after for her characters, even if there are a few road bumps along the way.

Today she lives in central Florida and writes full-time with the support of her loving husband and two finicky cats.

If you'd like to be notified of new releases, special sales, and get FREE ebooks, subscribe here: http://celiakyle.com/news

You can find Celia online at:

http://celiakyle.com

http://facebook.com/authorceliakyle

http://twitter.com/celiakyle

206

COPYRIGHT

CPSIA information can be obtained
at www.ICGtesting.com
Printed in the USA
LVHW11s1211071018
592719LV00001B/257/P